ABYSS

THE MYSTERIES OF
THE SEPTAGRAM

ABYSS

THE MYSTERIES OF THE SEPTAGRAM

PAUL BRYERS

Hodder
Children's
Books

A division of Hachette Children's Books

A Catalogue record for this book is available from the British Library

ISBN: 978 0 340 93077 9

Typeset in Bembo by Avon DataSet Ltd,
Bidford on Avon, Warwickshire

Printed and bound in Great Britain by
CPI Bookmarque Ltd, Croydon, Surrey

The paper and board used in this paperback by Hodder Children's Books
are natural recyclable products made from wood grown in sustainable
forests. The manufacturing processes conform to the environmental
regulations of the country of origin.

Hodder Children's Books
a division of Hachette Children's Books
338 Euston Road, London NW1 3BH
An Hachette UK company
www.hachette.co.uk

For Djinwenko and the children of Plan

1

Descent into Chaos

According to her teachers, Jade had a problem separating fantasy from reality. And at the moment, they seemed to have a point. For one thing, she didn't know where she was. And for another, she didn't know how she had got here.

It would help if she could see her surroundings, but she was in complete darkness: the darkness of a cave. Or a tomb.

It came to her that she was a vampire. This was a definite possibility. It was something she had been thinking rather a lot about lately. A vampire rising from the dead.

Suddenly it wasn't so dark any more and she was moving through trees on a mountain slope and she was aware that it was snowing. And in the distance there was a castle: a ruined castle in the snow.

Or perhaps it was ashes, falling from the leaden sky. Certainly there had once been a fire. There were dark stains on the ruined walls that looked like scorch marks. Or blood.

At first she thought it was deserted. Then she saw the monk. A monk all in black. He was standing on what remained of the ramparts and although she could not see his face – he was wearing a hood – she thought he was looking at her, waiting for her, and that he might have been waiting for some considerable time. Then as she approached he turned away and descended a flight of stone steps into a kind of courtyard, or what might once have been a room, now unroofed and open to the sky.

She followed him down the steps. She definitely had the impression of a descent, though she could not say for certain that it required any effort on her part. And now the monk was standing beside her and she distinctly heard him say: 'Which floor?'

Which floor???

It came to her then, perhaps a little later than it should have, that she was dreaming. And that it was probably going to be a bad dream.

This feeling became a certainty when the monk began to chant, tonelessly, like a lift-attendant in an old-fashioned department store.

'Ground floor: cosmetics, jewellery, ladies' lingerie, tights, toiletries, millinery, accessories and ladies' footwear.'

Jade expressed no preference and after a moment the descent continued.

'Upper basement: kitchenware, glassware, hardware, ceramics, electrical goods, household paints and DIY.'

None of these were of particular value or interest to Jade in her present situation – nor could she foresee a situation in the future when they ever would be – so she remained silent.

The next descent was longer and more alarming because the lift, if it *was* a lift, suddenly filled with smoke or dust and Jade thought she could smell burning. She looked to the monk for guidance or some expression of concern. She still could not see his face but she felt his eyes boring into her from the darkness under the hood.

Then, from the folds of his long black habit, he produced a tambourine, which he raised above his head and banged with the flat of his hand to make the bells ring.

Jade did not find this reassuring.

'I wish you would stop that,' she said firmly.

The monk took no notice. Instead, still banging the tambourine, he chanted: 'Lower basement: trolls, goblins, dwarves, dragons, wolves, bears, baboons and a few things I made myself.'

And then they stopped. And the lift doors opened and Jade stepped out into a large room. A cellar – or a dungeon? She could see chains on the walls and that mark again that could have been scorching, or rust, or blood. Then she saw the children. They advanced out of the shadows, children of about her own age who stood there watching her with their big eyes, not exactly filled with hope but as if they expected something of her. She felt that they were counting on her, but she did not know what they wanted, or how she was supposed to help them.

There was a light from above – it might even have been the sun pouring down through a hole in the roof – but there was so much smoke or dust, everything remained hazy and indistinct. And then the haze cleared a little, or Jade's eyes adjusted to it, and she saw there was a shape on the floor – a dark, huddled shape that could have been man or beast . . . And beside it was another hole. Like a well. Or something darker and much more terrible.

Then she had a dreadful sense of impending doom: a sense that something monstrous was about to happen, something that would change her life – and everything else – for ever. And she was powerless to stop it.

Then she was fighting her way upward, up through the darkness, struggling to reach the light and the air, knowing that she was trapped in a fearful nightmare and desperate to claw her way out of it.

And then she was awake. Eyes wide open in the dark. But not alone. There were others around her. She could hear them breathing, some murmuring in their sleep; one of them, quite close to her, whimpering softly.

And then it came to her, where she was. And she almost whimpered herself, almost wished herself back in the dream. Because no matter how terrible it was, it was a just a dream. A fantasy. But this was for real.

2

Punishment Time

I must not tell wicked lies, I must not tell wicked lies, I must not tell wicked lies . . .

Jade sat in the Great Hall at Saint Severa's, alone save for the aloof presence of Sister Beatrice at the far end of the room, and began the dreary process of filling in yet another page of her Punishment Book.

I must not tell wicked lies, I must not tell wicked lies . . .

Outside she could hear the distant voices of her fellow pupils playing hockey on the school fields and the faint harmonies of the choir at practice in the chapel. And, somewhat closer, the fretful drone of a bumblebee, as trapped as she was, struggling to reach light and air, doomed to fail.

Behind Sister Beatrice was a stained-glass window

showing the Day of Judgement, when the world came to an end and all the living and all the dead were rounded up to answer for their sins. There they all were, all the people of the world, lined up against a backdrop of ruined cities and burning forests and barren fields. And in the foreground was the Judgement, when they faced the Throne of God and were divided into two lines: one going off to the right through a golden door to Heaven, the other going off to the left, driven by demons with pitchforks, down the stairs to Hell: the fiery furnace where they would be punished for all eternity.

The meaning was clear, at least for Jade. If she carried on the way she was, this was where she was heading.

Saint Severa's was quite big on punishment. A modern school, it said in the prospectus, with old-fashioned values. Old-fashioned ideas about behaviour, and good manners, and discipline. Which was why Jade was sitting in the Great Hall under the watchful eye of Sister Beatrice writing *I must not tell wicked lies* one thousand times in her Punishment Book. After which she had to write a five-hundred-word essay entitled: '*Why Vampires Have No Basis in Reality*.'

Actually Sister Beatrice wasn't watching her. She was reading a book. Jade tried to see what it was but it was too far away to read the title. Probably not a book about vampires, though.

Jade liked reading. That's what she would have been doing during her recreation hour if she hadn't been writing one thousand lines. Sitting under one of the chestnut trees in the school grounds, reading a book and eating an apple. Taking in the last of the October sunshine. Instead of which . . .

I must not tell wicked lies, I must not tell wicked lies . . .

The lies were about vampires. Not vampire *bats*, which, as Jade could tell you, were a species of mammal that lived in parts of South America and fed on the blood of animals. But vampire *people*. Otherwise known as the Undead: human corpses that rose from the grave and fed on the blood of the living.

The girls who shared Jade's dormitory were familiar with stories about vampires, of course, but not with the stories Jade told them in the hour before lights out when they were supposed to be reading quietly, or praying, or composing themselves for sleep.

Jade told them that although vampires were supposedly from the land of Transylvania — a region of modern Romania in Eastern Europe — they could be found almost any place in the world, and although they were usually pictured as pale and thin with long fingernails, people who'd seen them said they were ruddy and bloated from all the blood they sucked, and they tended to vary in appearance from country to country like normal people. Bulgarian vampires had only one nostril; Bavarian vampires slept in the grave with their thumbs crossed and one eye open; Moravian vampires always attacked naked; and Albanian vampires wore high-heeled shoes.

Pressed by her audience, Jade threw in a few even more sensational details. Vampires from the Rocky Mountains in America sucked blood with their noses and only from the victim's ears. The greatest vampire of them all – Count Dracula – was based on a real-life prince of Romania called Vlad the Impaler who punished his enemies by dropping them on sharpened stakes that pierced them through the bottom and came out through their mouths. And yes – in answer to a question from Liza Becket – vampires still existed. And they had the power to change into something else entirely. They could change into bats, rats, black dogs and wolves, spiders, even moths. There could be one in the room now . . . What's that moving on the curtain?

For a brief period there was a secret cult of the vampire at Saint Severa's. Its acolytes practised certain rituals – nothing as extreme as Vlad the Impaler of course, that could not have gone unnoticed – but like the Bavarian vampires they slept with their thumbs crossed. They exchanged greetings by closing the left eye and pressing a finger against the right nostril. And when one of the school prefects passed them in the corridor or in the school grounds they drew in their bottom lip to reveal their fangs.

It was a game to most of them. A bit of harmless fun. But then one night Liza Becket woke up in the middle of the night screaming her head off and Jenny Rider wet the bed.

The Holy Inquisition quickly revealed the culprit. But Jade went on to compound the original sin, as they informed her, by telling the deputy head, Sister Margaret Clitherow, that it was all true. That there *were* such creatures as vampires in real life – or at least people *like* vampires, who did not die and could not be killed the way ordinary people were killed, but who could live for ever, unless someone shot them with a silver bullet or arrow or drove a stake through their hearts, or cut off their heads and filled their mouths with garlic.

'Where on earth did you learn such nonsense, child?' demanded the scandalized Sister Margaret Clitherow.

'It's just something I picked up,' replied Jade airily, 'in my travels.'

'In your travels indeed,' sneered the nun. 'Well, your travels are over, my girl. The only travelling you're going to be doing is to the Great Hall for Punishment Hour.'

I must not tell wicked lies, I must not tell wicked lies . . .

Jade put her hand up.

Sister Beatrice did not look up from her book.

Jade coughed politely.

Sister Beatrice sighed, carefully marked her place and looked at Jade over the top of her reading glasses.

'Yes?'

'Please, Sister, I've finished my lines.'

'Well, now you can start on your essay, can't you?'

'Well, as a matter of fact, Sister, I wanted to talk to you about that,' Jade informed her confidentially.

'Oh, did you, indeed? And what is there to talk about?'

'Well, it's just that, I've just written: *I must not tell wicked lies* a thousand times, right?'

Sister Beatrice frowned. 'Yes? And?'

'And now I've got to write an essay called –' she referred to the title she had been given '– *Why Vampires Have No Basis in Reality.*'

Sister Beatrice's frown grew deeper. 'Yes? And?'

'Well, if I believe there *are* such things as vampires and if I say there *aren't*, in this essay, I mean, I'd be lying, wouldn't I? At least as far as what *I* believe. You know?'

From the look Sister Beatrice was giving her, she didn't know. She didn't have the faintest idea what Jade was talking about but it sounded suspiciously like cheek. It sounded like someone was trying to put one over on her.

Jade tried to think of another way of putting it.

'I mean, it would be like making it worse, wouldn't it? Like "compounding the original sin".'

There were those who said that Jade was too clever by half. Too clever for her own good. And that everyone hated a smartypants. They had been saying this to her since she was about seven years old. She had learned to be more guarded in her opinions. But sometimes they just came out.

Sister Beatrice's voice was deceptively mild. 'Are you telling me you are not going to write this essay?'

'No-o,' mused Jade. 'I'm just saying I don't think it

would be *right* for me to write it. Not after writing: *I must not tell wicked lies* a thousand times. I don't mind writing another essay,' she offered helpfully. 'Like, "*Do Vampires Exist or not?*"'

'You will write the essay that you have been told to write . . .' The nun's voice was now cold and hard. 'And since you appear to know so much about the subject, you will write not five hundred words, but one thousand words.'

'But, Sister—'

'And if I have any more nonsense from you, you will write two thousand words. Do I make myself clear?'

Jade stared at her, outraged by the injustice. For a moment she considered dealing out her own form of punishment. But only for a moment. She had made a promise. And even if she *was* a wicked little liar, as Sister Margaret Clitherow had informed her, she was not the kind of person to break a promise.

So she took up her pen and started to write.

'*The trouble with vampires,*' she began, '*is that they assume many different forms so it is very difficult to know when you are in the presence of one. They have even been known to appear in the shape of quite holy people, like nuns. But the way you can always tell them is that they have no sense of humour – and very bad teeth . . .'*

This, she decided, could be a lot of fun.

It was almost dark when she came out of the Great Hall. People were drifting back from the playing fields, covered in mud and blood. A bit like vampires, newly risen from the grave.

Hockey, as played at Saint Severa's, was a dangerous game. The school, as well as being big on discipline, was also big on sports. Especially violent sports. Jade, who'd had quite enough of violence in her life, tried to avoid them as much as possible. She'd tried to avoid most things at Saint Severa's in the short time she had been here and as a result she had not made many friends. She had even fewer since the vampire business.

She was aware that many people thought she was stuck up – she was widely known as 'the princess' – and this distressed her. But what could she do? She was not stuck up. Just a bit shy and, if she were honest, a bit lost. Her last school had been a state school in west London and no one there had thought she was stuck up.

A psycho, maybe. But not stuck up.

She hadn't asked to be sent here. But certain people had decided it was in her 'best interests'.

That remained to be seen.

Jade looked about her as the sun sank beneath the Cumbrian Hills and darkness crept over the land. Saint Severa's was in the far north of England, about as far north as you could get, in fact, before you ran into Scotland. Border country.

In her history lessons Jade had learned about the border raiders, or reivers as they were called locally: the lawless families of cut-throats and brigands who lived on each side of the border and were forever raiding across it to steal cattle and whatever else they could lay their hands on – even women and children, who were then held for ransom. For hundreds of years they had engaged in blood feuds with rival clans. The history of the region was steeped in bloodshed and violence and treachery. A vampire would not have felt out of place here.

But it seemed peaceful enough now. Quite boring, in fact. A land of sheep farms and barren moorland and gently rolling foothills – called fells, from the Old Norse word for mountain, Sister Teresa had informed them in geography. Not that they were anything like real mountains: majestic giants with their heads in the clouds. More like trolls, to Jade's jaundiced eye, crouching under the pewter skies. A land of stunted trees and dry-stone walls covered with a sodden mat of moss and lichen. Why *dry* stone, when all it ever did was rain, Jade had asked when she first came here – before she learned not to ask questions that could be construed as *critical* – and was told it was because the walls were made without any mortar but by using stones that fitted together perfectly, like a jigsaw, and if she wanted to find out any more about the subject she could help the school caretaker mend one that had fallen down.

Certainly there was no shortage of stones to choose from. The hillsides were littered with them. Stones and sheep. Sometimes it was difficult to tell them apart, except that the sheep ran away when you got close to them and the stones stayed still.

The sheep seemed to be the only living creatures that could survive on the fells. Oh, and the hardy fell ponies – and the fierce black crows that nested in the gnarled old beech trees of the country churchyards and flew down to eat the afterbirths of the newborn lambs, and peck out their eyes if the ewes relaxed their wary vigilance.

It was not a land that Jade had learned to love.

The only things she liked about it were the rivers that issued from every crack and fissure in the grey-green hills and seemed always to be cheerful whatever the season.

It came to her one day that this was because they were on their way somewhere else.

So much for Cumbria. And as for the school . . .

The school occupied the site of an ancient castle perched on a crag above the River Eden. The ruins were still there, surrounded by barbed wire and warnings to Keep Out. This, Jade presumed, was the castle that haunted her dreams. It had once been the home of the Maxwells, one of the most feared of the reiver clans, but in more recent, less violent times they had built themselves a country house in the castle grounds and this was now Saint Severa's.

So far as Jade was concerned it was only slightly less forbidding than the castle, with its Gothic turrets and battlements and tall casement windows. As if the Maxwells hadn't been too sure the peace would hold and they'd be wise to sacrifice comfort for security.

Security was another thing they made a lot of at Saint Severa's.

'A school where pupils can learn to fulfil their true

potential in a safe, secure environment' it said in the prospectus.

People in the public eye, people with money and a position in society, could send their children to Saint Severa's secure in the knowledge that they would be kept out of harm's way, safe from kidnap and other misfortunes visited upon the rich and famous.

The Maxwells had chosen the site well. High on a ridge above the river, so they could see their enemies coming. And it wasn't the kind of landscape for creeping about in, not unless you disguised yourself as a sheep. Or a stone. Not the place for lingering with intent. A vehicle could be spotted several miles away; strangers were noticed. And the grounds were surrounded by a high stone wall. Not a dry-stone wall, either, but well-mortared and topped with razor wire. The massive wrought-iron gates were always firmly shut and could only be opened electronically by the security guards in the gatehouse. CCTV cameras scanned the approaches. Visitors were carefully checked before they were allowed in, and at night the guard dogs were released from their kennels and allowed to roam until dawn, savaging anything that moved.

There was some debate among the pupils of Saint Severa's as to whether all this was to keep intruders out or them in.

Jade had no illusions that it was the security aspect of Saint Severa's that had attracted the people responsible for her own welfare. That and the fact that the school had a reputation for coping with 'gifted' and 'difficult' children.

As for keeping her in, well, that was a different matter. She had escaped from more difficult places than this. But she had given her promise.

And a promise was a promise.

Still, she regretted it now as she made her way through the gloomy corridors to the refectory for the next ordeal of life at Saint Severa's.

Dinner.

For all the troubles of her past life — and there had been many — Jade had never had cause to complain about the food (as she would sometimes remark, with a significant glance towards the neck of whomsoever she happened to be talking to at the time, as if searching for the exact location of the carotid artery). But the food at Saint Severa's was appalling. Good, hearty fare, the nuns called it. Food for growing girls. Meat, potatoes and two veg — with never a trace of herbs or spices – and a great stodgy pudding to follow. Washed down with jugs of water.

'No wine?' Jade had queried on her first day, arching her brow. She had meant it to be ironic but this was probably when the princess thing started. Irony was not greatly appreciated at Saint Severa's. Certainly not from one of the younger girls. It was frequently confused with cheek.

They all stood for Grace, which was said by the principal, Sister Sarah, and about a second before it ended there was a great scraping of chairs and an eruption of excited chatter. But the atmosphere on Jade's table was subdued. Two of the younger girls had been part of the vampire cult and they studiously avoided Jade's eye. They were afraid of being associated with her in case they were hauled off to the dungeons and shown the instruments of torture. Jade had a good mind to give them the sign of recognition but she could feel Sister Margaret Clitherow glaring down at her from the high table and there was no point in provoking further punishment.

There were two senior girls on each table who acted as servers. They collected the food in containers from the serving hatches and brought it to the tables and dished it out to the younger girls. The two servers on Jade's table were called Rose and Jasmine. They had a bit of a double act going but in Jade's opinion they weren't half as funny as they thought they were – except to look at. Jasmine was tall and thin with a long sharp nose, all elbows and knees. Rose was a great lump of a girl with a round red face and lots of chins.

Jade watched them carefully as they dished out the portions and passed them down the table. They worked very fast but they made sure they kept back more than enough for themselves. Jade wasn't wild about the food at Saint Severa's but it added insult to injury to be done out of your fair share.

She stared at the miserable offering laid before her. A mound of greyish-white mashed potato rising out of a pool of brown minced meat with a few shreds of onion floating in it, like fingernails. Shepherd's pie – a Saint Severa's staple. They had it at least once a week, sometimes twice. Jade had put it about that the school had a deal going with the local farmer for all the sheep that had died on the roads.

'The princess doesn't look very happy today,' said Jasmine.

'The princess never looks happy,' said Rose. 'I expect

she misses the champagne and caviar at the palace.'

'Oh, that's not all,' said Jasmine. 'She usually has a nice drink of blood about this time of the day, don't you, Princess? Needs her blood, our little princess,' she informed Rose confidentially, 'or she goes all pale and woozy.'

'What you talking about?' demanded Rose, staring at Jade with suspicion – and perhaps a hint of fear. 'What blood?'

Doesn't like the thought of blood. Jade made a mental note and stored it away for future reference.

'Oh, haven't you heard? The princess thinks she's a vampire. She goes flitting about after lights out taking a bite here, a bite there. Otherwise she'd just waste away, wouldn't you, Princess?'

'Which is not something you'll ever have to worry about, is it?' murmured Jade, just loud enough for the girls on each side to hear but not to reach the two servers at the head of the table. They could tell it was something clever though from the hastily suppressed grins.

'What was that?' Rose scowled fiercely. 'Come on, if it's that funny you can share it with all of us.'

'I said I don't suppose there's any salt and pepper about, is there?' said Jade innocently.

The two girls glared down the table at her.

'I think someone needs taking down a peg or two,' said Jasmine menacingly. 'I think someone needs to learn the meaning of respect.'

Jasmine always talked like Sister Margaret Clitherow.

Jade put her head down and dug her fork into the mound of mashed potato.

How long could she bear it?

'*See how you like it,*' her Aunt Em had said. '*If you're very unhappy, well, we can talk again but let's give it a fair crack of the whip.*'

Unfortunate expression in the circumstances.

But she had agreed to give it a go. Aunt Em thought it wouldn't do her any harm to be treated as if she wasn't so very special. And maybe she was right. She knew she didn't behave very well sometimes.

Besides, where else could she go? No one seemed terribly keen on having her live with them. And at least she was safe, comparatively speaking. There were enough crucifixes at Saint Severa's to keep out a whole army of vampires.

Pity there wasn't a bit more garlic. It might give a bit of taste to the food.

She chewed her way through the shepherd's pie

and washed it down with several glasses of water. For pudding they had what the cook called jam roly-poly but the girls called dead man's leg because that's what it looked like. Jade ate a few mouthfuls just to keep her strength up. She reckoned from the looks she was getting from the head of the table that she would need it, sooner or later.

She didn't have long to wait.

She was walking back down the corridor towards her dorm when she felt a flabby hand on her shoulder. It was Rose, with Jasmine lurking in the background. The other girls melted away as if by magic.

'A word,' said Rose.

'If it's not too much trouble,' said Jasmine with a sneer.

'Well, as a matter of fact, I've got work to do,' said Jade, 'so if you don't mind . . .' She tried to shrug off the restraining hand but the grip tightened.

'In here,' said Jasmine opening the door into an empty classroom.

Rose swung Jade around and pushed her in.

3

Fire and Blood

Jasmine closed the door and twisted the knob to lock it. Then she pulled down the blind — only ever used if one of the teachers wanted to play a DVD or something. But this was probably not what the two girls had in mind. Jade was determined not to show fear. She sat down at one of the desks.

'So what can I do for you?' she said calmly.

'Who told you to sit down?' demanded Rose. She turned to Jasmine. 'Did you tell her to sit down?'

'I didn't tell her to sit down,' said Jasmine. 'Stand up,' she snarled at Jade.

Jade stayed sitting. 'Come on,' she said. 'Get it off your chest. I haven't got all night.'

Jasmine went a shade paler. She stepped right up to

Jade, drew her hand back and slapped her as hard as she could right across the face.

Jade gasped. She put her hand up to her burning cheek. It stung but the humiliation was worse. Her eyes narrowed. She looked at Jasmine very carefully and concentrated hard.

'Don't you look at me like that,' said Jasmine. She drew her arm back to slap Jade again. But then a strange expression crossed her face. She looked at her hand. Then she let out a strange bleating noise and began to flap her hand about wildly in the air as if something was sticking to it.

'What are you doing?' demanded Rose in astonishment. 'Jasmine?'

'Aaah, aaah, aaah!' yelped Jasmine. She started to run around in small circles, slapping her right hand with her left hand and keeping up that weird wailing, like a kind of war dance except that she didn't look very fierce. She looked terrified.

'Put it out!' she yelled. 'Put it out!'

'Put what out?' Rose looked around the room in alarm.

'The fire, the fire!' screamed Jasmine. She began to bang her hand on the nearest desk as hard as she could.

'What fire?' Rose was still looking around the room. Then she saw what Jasmine was doing. 'Stop it,' she implored her urgently. 'You'll hurt yourself.' She looked at Jade with fear in her eyes. 'What's wrong with her?'

'She thinks her hand's on fire,' said Jade. She put her own hand up to her forehead and began to massage it gently to ease the headache she felt coming on.

'But – it isn't.'

'I know that, you know that . . .' Jade sighed. 'But she seems to think it is.'

They both looked at the hysterical girl. She stopped banging the desk and made a dash for the door, fumbling to open it with her left hand, but she was in too much of a panic. She collapsed to the floor, rolling around and wailing and blowing on her hand.

'What can I do?' Rose anguished. 'Jasmine, tell me what to do.'

'You could call the fire brigade, I suppose,' Jade suggested thoughtfully, as Jasmine clearly wasn't coming up with any ideas. 'But they'll be half an hour coming from Penrith. If I was you I'd fetch a bucket of water.'

Rose turned on her. 'You little monster,' she hissed. 'What have you done to her?' She advanced towards Jade threateningly.

'You're bleeding,' said Jade.

'What?'

'There's blood on your cheek.'

Rose put a hand up to her face and then took it away and held it in front of her with a look of horror.

'Blood!' she said faintly.

Jade saw her face go pale and her eyes start to roll back in her head. She managed to guide her to a chair before she passed out.

'Put your head between your knees,' Jade instructed her.

Then she crossed over to the other girl, took hold of her wrist and raised her hand to her lips as if she was going to kiss it. She blew gently.

'There – I've put it out,' she said. 'Now go and stick it in cold water for half an hour.'

Then she crossed to the door, twisted the handle to free the lock, and walked out into the corridor. She could feel the most incredible headache coming on and with it a terrible sense of guilt. All she wanted to do was lie down in a darkened room.

'There you are! I've been looking for you all over the place.'

Jade turned, bracing herself for more trouble. But it was Sister Martha, one of the youngest nuns at Saint Severa's and one of the kindest.

'There's a phone call for you,' she said, 'in the school office. If they haven't hung up by now.'

The girls weren't allowed mobile phones in school. They had to book calls from the phones in the school office – and only for five minutes at a time. Incoming calls were not encouraged, unless there was an emergency, or some vital family matter to be discussed. So it was with some concern that Jade hurried to the office to pick up the waiting call.

'Jade – are you all right?'

It was her Aunt Em.

'Yes,' said Jade wonderingly. 'Why? What's up? Has something happened?'

'No – but I've just had a call from Sister Sarah.'

'Really?' Jade injected a note of surprise into her voice. It didn't sound very convincing, even to her.

'She wants me to come and see her – as if it's just round the corner and not at the far end of England.'

Tell me about it, thought Jade.

'Oh?' she said. 'What for?'

'You mean you don't know?'

'No. She hasn't said anything to me.'

'Jade, you haven't been up to anything, have you?'

'Me?'

'You know what I mean. You haven't been up to any of your old tricks?'

'I'm sorry?' Jade still managed to sound mystified and faintly indignant. 'What tricks?'

It was far too early for Jasmine to have gone running to Sister Sarah. Besides, what was she going to tell her? *I slapped Jade Connor across the face and my hand went on fire . . .*

'You know very well what tricks,' said Aunt Em sternly.

Jade said nothing.

'Well, I can only come at the end of the week,' Aunt Em resumed.

'You're coming up here?'

'That's what I've just said, isn't it? I'll find out about the trains – but it probably won't be until Saturday afternoon.' There was a short pause. 'I'll book in at a hotel in Appleby and perhaps on Sunday we can go out for lunch or something. Provided you're not grounded.' Another pause. 'Jade?'

'Yes? I'm still here.'

'Are you sure you're all right?'

'Yes,' Jade said. 'I'm fine.'

But when the call ended she felt a terrible sense of loneliness, even greater than the loneliness she felt most of the time. Her relations with Aunt Em were a bit strained at times. Which was why she always thought of her as 'Aunt Em' – or simply 'Em' like the head of the secret service in James Bond – never 'Auntie' or 'Auntie Emily'. She wasn't actually Jade's aunt: she was her godmother. And not even that, technically speaking, because Jade hadn't ever been christened. But there had always been something of a bond between them, even if it was difficult to pin down what it was exactly. People said they were very alike. Jade couldn't see that, though she wouldn't have minded if they were because her Aunt Em was generally regarded as quite stunningly beautiful – and exceptionally talented. She was a doctor – Dr Emily Mortlake, followed by a string of letters – and she worked for the government. Her speciality was genetics, which she had once described to Jade as 'the code that holds the secret of human life.'

That was about as much as Jade knew about Aunt Em's work and as much as she wanted to know. And as for her private life, that was a bit of a mystery, too.

So far as Jade knew she hadn't ever married, she didn't seem to have any boyfriends, or any friends at all. She said she never had the time. But recently she seemed to have become more involved in Jade's affairs – or at least with the decisions that affected her life. In fact, in some ways she seemed to be running the show. Probably because there was no one else willing to do it. Not any more. Her foster parents seemed to have dropped out of the picture entirely – and she couldn't really blame them, the way she had behaved.

Jade emerged from the office and made her way back towards the dormitories. The headache had faded somewhat but she could still feel it lurking between her eyes, like a mugger waiting to pounce when she least expected it. And the sense of guilt was worse. She had broken a promise. Worse, she had used her powers to punish people. They might have asked for it but that wasn't good enough. She had behaved like her father and she hated herself for it. Then she saw Jasmine and Rose again. Jasmine was kneeling on the floor with her arm plunged into one of the fire buckets and Rose was slumped next to her with her back against the wall and her legs stretched out into the corridor. And Sister Martha was standing over them demanding to know what was going on.

Jade thought it best not to get involved.

She did a smart about-turn and headed back the way she had come. But she was just passing the office again when she heard voices from the floor below. One of them sounded oddly familiar. Jade leaned over the balcony and saw the head teacher with a younger woman – not a nun by the look of her. She was wearing a smart belted raincoat and boots and a black beret. And she looked vaguely familiar.

They were crossing the lobby towards the front door but it was difficult to make out her features. The lighting was so bad at Saint Severa's, they might as well use candles. But then Sister Sarah opened the door and the light spilled in from the lamp in the porch and at the same moment the woman raised her head.

Jade gasped and pressed herself back against the wall. The blood had drained from her face. Anyone seeing her would have thought she had seen a ghost. And perhaps she had.

They had found her.

But *how*?

It didn't matter. The only thing that mattered was that they had found her – and it would take more than a high wall and a few guard dogs and several hundred crucifixes to keep them out.

4

The Devil's Daughter

The woman Jade knew as 'Aunt Em' arrived at Saint Severa's just as the last of the light drained from the northern sky. She had been travelling for most of the day. Five hours in the train from London and another hour in the hire car she had picked up at the station. She was not in the best of moods. She had lost her way several times since leaving Penrith and she was already a quarter of an hour late for her appointment with the head teacher.

'Just follow the signs for Long Marton,' they'd said, 'then turn right after you cross a humpbacked bridge and you'll see the ruins of the old castle on a crag above the river.'

But there weren't any signs for Long Marton.

None she could find, anyway, and no one to give her any directions. The few scattered hill farms she passed were a long way back from the road and seemed entirely devoid of human life. The only living things in sight were the distant sheep and a few crows eating something that had died by the side of the road. But after following a narrow winding lane for several miles, Emily spotted the ruined castle. In the gathering dusk it appeared to beckon her like the finger of doom. How could she ever have agreed to send Jade to such a place? She must have been out of her mind.

No, just your usual selfish, self-regarding, self-centred self, said a sardonic voice inside her head, the voice of her conscience.

Oh, shut up, she told it, *what else was I to do? Give up my career, live in a fortress, employ an army of bodyguards . . . ?*

The voice was silent – for the time being.

She drove up to the school gates. They were closed.

She leaned on the horn. It sounded like a sheep bleating.

The gates stayed closed.

With a sigh she stepped out of the car. There was an entry-phone set into one of the gateposts. A set of numbers for some code she didn't know and a single button with a sign that said: *Press and Wait*. She pressed and waited. The wind sighed through the razor wire on top of the walls. The scudding clouds threatened more rain. A CCTV camera watched her through its cold Cyclops eye. A distant, muffled voice invited her to identify herself. She leaned into the microphone.

'Dr Emily Mortlake,' she said, raising her voice to compete with the wind. 'I have an appointment with the head teacher.'

For a moment nothing; then, with an eerie electric hum, the gates swung open.

Emily got back into the car and drove through. A long narrow driveway stretched ahead of her with fields on either side, much the same as the fields she had been driving through for the past hour or so except that there were no sheep. Through the rear-view mirror she watched the gates close behind her. Then, after a few hundred metres she reached another barrier, just a single metal bar this time, beside a stone keeper's lodge. A uniformed security guard emerged and requested proof of identity.

Emily showed him her security pass from the Ministry.

'Follow the signs to the visitors' car park,' he told her, 'and report to the school office.'

All very military, but she could hardly complain about that. That was the main reason Jade was here. She drove on up to the school, as grim in its way as the ruined keep, but at least there were a few lights on in the windows. She wondered if Jade was looking out for her. Or even that she might come running to meet her. But that wasn't Jade's style, not lately at any rate.

She ignored the signs to the visitors' car park and parked the car as close as possible to the main entrance, combed her fingers through her short blonde hair, thought about freshening up her lipstick, decided against it on the grounds that nuns probably didn't care one way or another, and sallied forth to do battle with Sister Sarah.

'Ah, Dr Mortlake . . . So you managed to find us.'

When Emily had seen Sister Sarah's name in the school prospectus – with a stream of academic qualifications after it – she had imagined a scholarly nun in a blue headscarf, a woman of sharp intellect but gentle manner. The reality was a formidable bruiser in her mid-fifties who looked as if she would be equally at home presiding over a board meeting in the City of London, or striding about the playing fields of Saint Severa's like the Duchess in *Alice in Wonderland* belting a croquet ball with a flamingo and bawling, 'Off with her head.' She wore a tweed suit and a crisp white blouse and the only visible sign of her calling was a small silver crucifix on a chain around her neck. Emily found herself babbling an apology about her late arrival and 'getting lost driving out of Penrith'.

'Yes, it is a little confusing if you're not used to it,' said Sister Sarah briskly, as if her visitor had dropped in from outer space or just been let out of an institute for the aged and infirm. 'You should have taken a taxi. It's only a few miles.'

Fifteen actually, Emily felt like saying, but instead she just gave a little smile and a shrug. In fact she had picked up a hire car because she didn't know how long she would be kept hanging about or even whether she would end up taking Jade back with her. Having her own car gave her more of a sense of control. At least, until she got lost.

'Well, now you're here, do make yourself comfortable.' Sister Sarah indicated one of the stiff straight-backed chairs opposite her desk, which looked about as comfortable as a ducking stool for witches. 'Can I offer you tea or coffee?'

'No thank you, Sister.' Emily sat down, crossing her legs coolly to let the nun know she was not one of her pupils. It didn't entirely work. She wore a black woollen business suit by Peruvian Connection and a pair of Prada folded boots in black suede but she felt as if she was ten years old and had been summoned straight from the hockey field in her muddy gym kit to receive a severe ticking off for idleness. In fact she had never been ticked off at her own school – for idleness or anything else. She had been a perfect student from start to finish and had ended up head girl. But she had always been striving for approval, always fearful of rebuke, or of failing to live up to her own high standards. The interview with Sister Sarah reminded her of this.

Get a grip, she instructed herself sternly. She had come a long way since her schooldays and was not noted for timidity. Even her superiors at the Ministry were frightened of her. She wasn't going to be bossed about by a nun – even a nun built to the proportions of Sister Sarah.

'So.' The head teacher leaned forward, folding her massive arms across the desk and thrusting her chin forward like a pit bull scenting a fight. 'I'm sorry to have to drag you up here at such short notice but I'm afraid Jade has not settled in quite as we would have wished.'

'Oh.' Emily frowned as if this was difficult to believe, though in fact she could believe it only too well. 'What exactly is the problem?'

'More a case of problems, I regret to say.' Sister Sarah consulted, or pretended to consult, the papers on her desk. 'Has she ever had any trouble with vampires?'

'Excuse me?'

'Bats,' explained Sister Sarah. 'Though Jade's interest appears to be in the mythical variety. Loathsome creatures that she calls the Undead. She even seems to have founded some kind of secret society. A cult of the vampire, one might say.'

'Well, I'm very sorry but—'

'And I'm afraid that's not all. She has informed several people that her father is a criminal mastermind who is being pursued by the police on several continents. She is not even consistent in her fantasies. She told one girl that he was a vampire and another that he was the Devil — which would make her the Devil's daughter. Such an illusion is not encouraged, Dr Mortlake, in a Catholic school for girls. She said that until recently she lived with him in a castle in Lapland with a pet bear and a variety of more exotic creatures, some of which he had made himself, until he was attacked by reindeer herders and flew away in a balloon in the general direction of Russia.'

Emily frowned. 'That is a little fanciful, I agree . . .'

'Only a little?' The head teacher's tone was mocking. This was unfortunate. Emily did not like being mocked. Or bullied. It provoked her into saying more than she had intended.

'Well, I didn't see the bear myself but I am assured plenty of people did. And although I personally don't believe in the Devil I'm told others do.'

'I gather you are not inclined to take this seriously,' snapped the nun.

'Oh, I take it very seriously. And so do the police. On several continents.'

'You are telling me that Jade's father is wanted by the police?'

Emily realized that this wasn't helping.

'I'm not sure why this is relevant . . .' she began, but the nun was rooting among her paperwork.

'On the application form it clearly states that

Jade was brought up by foster parents living in west London and that you, Dr Mortlake, are now her legal guardian . . .'

'That's true, though actually, the legal guardians are the courts . . .'

The head teacher looked up in astonishment. 'The courts?'

'Jade was made a ward of court, to protect her from her father, but I have the responsibility for her care and protection . . .'

'And I have the responsibility for the care and protection of the pupils of Saint Severa's,' insisted the head teacher angrily.

'One of whom is Jade,' Emily pointed out. 'And I was assured that she would be safe here. Indeed, if it had not been for the recommendation of a certain person in Holy Orders I would never have agreed to send her here.'

The head teacher sighed. This also was in the paperwork. Indeed, Jade's application had been supported by several senior figures in the Church, including her own superiors.

'Let's have her in and see what she has to say for herself,' she said. She pressed a button on her intercom. 'Be so good as to send Jade Connor into my office,' she instructed her secretary. 'You will find her waiting in the school library.'

But Jade was not waiting in the school library.

'We cannot find her,' announced the secretary, standing in the doorway and wringing her hands. 'We have searched the entire school and we cannot find her anywhere.'

5

The Runaway

Emily waited alone in the head teacher's study. It had been half an hour now and still no word. She wondered if she should take some action on her own account – but what? She stood up and walked to the window for about the tenth time, pressing her nose against the glass and making a tunnel with her hands to cut out the reflections. But it was darker now and all she could see was a small patch of empty playground. A flurry of rain spattered against the window pane.

Where could she be? And on such a night. She surely would not have gone out in this. She had to be somewhere in the school. But why did she not wait in the library as she was told?

The door opened and Emily turned expectantly – but it was only the head teacher, and she was shaking her head.

'We can't find her,' she admitted. She crossed to her desk and threw herself heavily into her chair.

'But this is ridiculous,' said Emily.

'Quite.' The head teacher spread her hands as if to say, look what we have to put up with.

'Could she have left the school grounds?'

'Impossible. The gates are locked. She couldn't climb the walls, not without assistance. Or a ladder. Unless she is able to fly. Besides, the dogs are loose. Only a fool would go out there after dark.'

The dogs are loose. What kind of school *was* this?

'And if she did go out there –' Emily gestured angrily towards the window '– what would the dogs do to her?'

'Oh, they'll only bark at her but they won't let her move until the security guards arrive. They're trained not to harm the girls,' Sister Sarah assured her. 'Only outsiders.'

Charming.

'Even so, shouldn't we be calling the police?'

'Good heavens! That would be a little extreme, wouldn't it? She's only been gone half an hour.'

'Yet you can't find her.'

Sister Sarah closed her eyes briefly as if she felt a migraine coming on. 'She's probably hiding from you,' she said.

Emily's voice rose. 'Hiding? From me? Why on earth should she be hiding from me?'

'I've really no idea,' said Sister Sarah wearily. 'Perhaps she thought you would be angry with her. I expect she'll come out soon enough. When you've gone.'

'*When I've gone*?' Emily couldn't believe this. 'You seriously expect me to leave here without seeing her – or knowing what has happened to her?'

Sister Sarah looked uncomfortable. Her hand reached uncertainly for the telephone on her desk. But then it dropped back.

'Were you planning to stay the night up here,' she enquired, 'or travel straight back to London?'

'I'm booked in at the Royal Oak in Appleby,' Emily informed her coldly. 'I *had* thought of taking Jade out for the day – if that's permitted.'

Sister Sarah made a steeple with her fingers. 'I'm afraid after this little incident we really will have to consider Jade's position here,' she said.

'I have already considered it and come to my own

conclusions,' Emily replied sharply.

'Quite. Well, in the meantime, I suggest you make your way to the hotel and I will make sure you are informed as soon as the girl chooses to present herself. You can come to collect her in the morning and you can rest assured she will be ready and waiting for you. With her bags packed.'

Emily was still fuming as she drove through the school gates. Her mind was full of all the things she wished she had said to the woman – nun or no nun – but they would have to keep until the morning. The important thing was to collect Jade and her belongings and get her away from here before anything else happened. She could hardly believe she had let her come here in the first place.

The rain swept across the road ahead, dense in the beam of the car headlights. It was a filthy night. She peered through the windscreen and turned the demister on to full blast. Then, above the whirr of the fan and the swish of the windscreen wipers she heard another noise. A knocking noise.

'Oh, no,' she said aloud. 'Not now. Not here.'

All she needed was a breakdown. For all her knowledge of genetics and the human body, Emily was woefully ignorant when it came to motor cars. The noise was getting worse. She pulled on to the grass verge and switched off the engine. But the knocking continued. And there was another sound, a kind of . . . squeaking.

'Good grief!'

Emily leaped out of the car and yanked open the boot.

'About time,' said an indignant voice. 'Couldn't you hear me?'

'Jade! What on earth . . . ?'

Jade screwed her face up against the rain.

'Do you think we could talk about it in the car?' she suggested.

They sat in the front seats with the rain beating against the windows.

'Can you turn the heater on?' Jade requested after she had given her godmother a few moments to compose herself with her head slumped on the wheel. 'It was freezing in the back there.'

Emily raised her head and glared at her. 'You shouldn't have been in the back there,' she pointed out. 'What do you think you're playing at?'

'Well, if I'd sat in the front they'd have seen me, wouldn't they?'

'And what makes you think they'd have stopped you? As a matter of fact the head teacher was about to expel you.'

'Oh? Well, I wasn't going to take any chances,' Jade muttered darkly.

'Honestly, Jade. Nothing's ever simple with you, is it? Put your seatbelt on.'

'Why? Where we going?'

'Back to the school. So I can tell them I've found you and they can stop searching. And then you are going to pack your bags and we're going to leave like civilized human beings and stay the night in Appleby. At an hotel.'

'I've already packed my bags. They're in the boot.'

'I see. Well . . .' Emily struggled to put her thoughts in order. 'Even so, we have to let Sister Sarah know where you are and then—'

'OK, phone her then.'

'What?'

'Phone her. Tell her you found me wandering in the school grounds. But don't tell her *where* we've gone,' she added. 'I mean, don't tell her which hotel we're staying at.'

'Why on earth not?'

'Because you can't trust her.'

'Excuse me?'

'I saw her with Barmella.'

'Who?'

'You know. Barmella.' She pronounced her full name. 'Countess Sophie Caroline Maria Baer-Mellor von Koffen. The human bone-cruncher. If she *is* human. The muscle machine. The killer countess. The leg-breaker in leotards.'

'Jade, what on earth are you talking about?'

'The woman who works for *him*.'

'*Him?*' Emily frowned. 'You mean . . .'

'You know who I mean.' She couldn't bring herself to say his name. Besides, it was dangerous. He might hear you.

'And you saw her with Sister Sarah?'

'Yes. She was wearing a disguise but I'd know her anywhere. They've found me again.'

Emily shook her head. 'I don't know what to think.' She reached for her phone in the holdall between the two front seats. 'But I've got to phone the school or they'll be searching for you all night.'

'So what are you going to tell them?'

'The truth. I know you find that distressing but sometimes it's the best thing to do.'

'But you're not going to take me back?'

'No, I'm not going to take you back. We'll stop the night in Appleby and tomorrow we'll take the train back to London.'

'Yes!' Jade punched the air in triumph.

Emily sighed. 'And then we'll work out what to do next.'

She started to search for the number of the school. But then the headlights of a car appeared on the road ahead. They were on full beam and she raised her hand to shield her eyes until the car had passed. But Jade had twisted in her seat to look back.

'They've stopped,' she said.

Emily saw the red brake lights in the driving mirror.

'They're turning round,' cried Jade in alarm.

'Perhaps they think we're broken down.' But her voice was uncertain.

'Drive on!' Jade commanded her urgently. 'Please. It's him. I know it is. Drive! Now!'

Emily swung out into the road.

'They'll stop when they see we're OK,' she said.

But they didn't stop. They kept on coming, the headlights on full beam, filling the car interior with their menacing glare.

6

The Car Chase

'Faster, faster,' yelled Jade, twisting round in the seat and shielding her eyes from the glaring headlights. 'He's right up your bum.'

'Jade!' Emily crouched over the steering wheel, peering through the frantically swishing blades of the windscreen wipers.

'He's on your tail, then. Whatever. Just move it!'

'This is ridiculous,' moaned Emily. 'He's probably lost and wants to ask the way.'

'Sure, and I'm the Wicked Witch of the West.'

'Tell me something I don't know already.'

'Funny. Well, if you're so sure it's not him, pull over and ask him where he wants to go to.'

Emily didn't reply. But she didn't pull over, either.

'He's trying to overtake – hard right, hard right,' screamed Jade. Then she turned round and saw another bend coming up. 'Look out! Hard left!'

Emily wrenched at the wheel and they rode up on the grass verge, the wheels spinning helplessly before they lurched back on to the road.

'Jade, will you shut up and let me do the driving,' Emily snapped at her.

'OK but whatever you do, don't let him into your head.'

'What do you mean by that?'

'Keep your eyes on the road! You know what I mean. Don't let him into your head.'

'I *don't* know what you mean. Even if it *is* him – and I don't for a moment believe it is – how can he get into my head?'

'He just can. Trust me. He'll make you stop or go skidding off the road. He'll try and get into mine, too. You have to make your mind a complete blank.'

'Yes, well you probably find that a lot easier than I do.'

'Ha, ha.' But then the interior of the car was filled with light as their pursuer closed on them again and Jade put her hands up to her head. 'He's trying, I can feel it. Go away! La, la, la, not taking any notice, la la la, not listening.' She began to sing at the top of her voice: *'Hallelujah! Hallelujah! Hallelujah!'* Then in a deeper tone: *'Hallelujah! Hallelujah!'*

'What are you doing?' Emily shot her a look of total astonishment.

'Singing the Hallelujah Chorus,' Jade informed her reasonably. 'It's by Handel. We sing it at school.'

'Well, don't sing it here. I don't find it very helpful. Oh, my God!' She hit the brakes as they went into the next bend.

'It keeps him out of your head,' Jade explained. 'You should sing too. Anything you like but hymns are best. He hates hymns. Or Christmas carols. Anything religious. It doesn't have to be complicated. The simpler the better.'

She raised her voice again:

'Twinkle, twinkle little star,
How I wonder what you are.'

They skidded round the bend and went straight into another. Emily wrestled desperately with the wheel.

'Up above the world so high,
Like a diamond in the sky . . .'

Emily glanced in the mirror. The car was still hot on their tail.

'Look out!' Jade yelled. 'The bridge!'

But it was too late. The bridge seemed to leap at them through the curtain of rain – the humpbacked bridge over the River Eden that Emily had searched for in vain on the way to Saint Severa's. She didn't see it this time either. They hit it at about 50 miles an hour and took off. But not for long. They came down with a bone-shaking thud and a tortured shriek of rubber. Even then they might have made it if Emily hadn't slammed on the brakes. The car skidded violently into the dry-stone wall, burst through into the field beyond, rolled over twice, paused for a moment the right way up and then slid slowly down the bank into the swollen river.

And the black rushing waters closed over them.

7

The Warrior Monks

Rome. Seven in the evening. And strangely deserted, at least in the squares and walkways of the Vatican, though elsewhere the traffic snarled and hooted with its usual level of impotent fury. But few pedestrians cared to brave the rain that poured down from the black clouds, surging through the gutters and exploding like shotgun pellets on the sluggish waters of the River Tiber.

The stone angels on the Ponte Sant'Angelo watched impassively as a solitary figure sprinted across the bridge towards the floodlit bulk of the Castello that towered above the further end: a hooded figure in black leather jacket and jeans, his trainers splashing through the puddles in his haste to reach the shelter of the ancient fortress.

A sentry emerged from the shadows of the gatehouse as the figure approached – for it was well past closing time and hooded figures were suspect, unless, of course, they wore the robes of antiquity, like the monks and friars of this sainted city. The sentry himself wore the traditional striped uniform of the Swiss Guard, famed defenders of the Papacy for over five hundred years, and the only weapon he carried was an ancient pike. The runner stopped and reached into an inside pocket for his pass, pushing back his hood to reveal the features of a young man, probably in his late twenties, with a stubble of beard and longish blond hair.

The guard scrutinized the pass in the light of the great wrought-iron lantern hanging above the gateway.

Brother Benedict Ullman, he read, *Knight of the Order of Saint Saviour of Antioch*.

A flicker of surprise crossed the sentry's face.

'Fra Benedicta?' he pronounced uncertainly.

'That's me,' said the man cheerfully.

'Knight?'

An inclination of the head and an apologetic grin. The sentry glanced once more at the document.

It bore the crest of the Vatican and was signed by the right authorities with a photograph that pretty much resembled the man standing in front of him. He returned the pass and stood aside with a jerk of his head.

'Thank you,' said Brother Benedict. He pulled up his hood and jogged on into the interior of the castle.

The sentry watched him go with a puzzled frown. He saw many monks in the course of his duties but none dressed like that and none who went by the title of Knight. He supposed it must be one of the military orders, a bit like his own. But the monk appeared very young to have attained such seniority – though there had been something about his eyes, now the sentry came to think about it, that seemed older . . .

He shuddered suddenly, as if chilled by the rain, and stepped back into the shelter of the gatehouse.

The monk ran on through the silent courtyards of the ancient citadel, his shadow dancing before him on the shining wet stones. Above him rose the single massive tower of the fortress with its distinctive bronze angel perched on the roof – the Archangel Michael, no less, who had expelled Adam and Eve from the Garden of Eden and closed the gates with his burning sword, and guarded them still against the trespass of humankind.

The angel was there for a particular reason. Legend had it that in the year 590 AD – which was then almost five hundred years after the fortress had been built – the city had been afflicted by a terrible plague and the Pope of that day had led a procession through the streets to pray for deliverance. Then, as he led his followers across the bridge towards the castle, he looked up to behold the archangel standing on the roof, sheathing his sword as a sign that the plague had ended and the city was spared.

Since then the Castel Sant'Angelo had served the Popes as a fortress, guarding the northern approaches to the city, a refuge in times of danger, and a vault for their treasures. But it also had a more sinister reputation as a prison.

For many centuries the courtyards through which Benedict now ran had been stained with the blood of countless executions, and in the dark, damp cells that surrounded them many hundreds of prisoners had died of hunger and thirst and despair.

The castle was now a museum but, unknown to the hoards of tourists who flocked here in the summer season, unknown to most of the churchmen and women who lived and worked in the Vatican – known in fact only to a very small circle of cardinals and advisers to the Pope – it was the headquarters of one of the most secretive societies in this city of secrets.

The Knights of Saint Saviour had been formed in the twelfth century to defend Jerusalem against the Saracens and other enemies of the Church and to protect the pilgrims who journeyed there from all over Christendom. They had been driven from the Holy Land by the armies of Saladin and had roamed Europe for many years as homeless mercenaries and errant knights fighting for whoever would employ them. They had fought for the Kings of Hungary and the Emperors of Austria and Germany, moving ever northward, until they managed to carve out an empire of their own in the lands fringing the Baltic Sea, an empire that in time had extended as far north as Finland and the borders of Arctic Russia.

Long after they had lost their lands and riches and their armies had been defeated and disbanded they had continued to serve the Church as envoys and spies and even, though less frequently, as soldiers. Like the angel on the roof, they had only part-sheathed the sword and were always ready to draw it in the service of their historic masters.

Brother Benedict reached the main gate of the fortress and was once more required to show his pass before the sentry permitted him to enter the inner sanctum. Slowing down to a walk, he crossed a stone-flagged lobby and mounted the stairs to the third floor, showed his pass again and navigated his way confidently through the maze of corridors until he reached a locked door with a sign that read: *Private: No Unauthorized Admission*. Undeterred, Benedict slid his security pass into the slot on the wall, tapped a series of numbers into the metal keypad, and entered a long, narrow chamber equipped with metal lockers and wooden benches, like the changing room of a gym.

Five minutes later he emerged in a long black robe with a white cross at the shoulder, his features hidden by a long, tapering hood or cowl. He continued along several corridors until he reached another door, which opened directly into a high-ceilinged chamber about the size of a large dining room, lit by a single chandelier with seven flickering candles. Beneath the chandelier was a round table divided into seven segments, radiating outwards like the wedges of a cheese, and at the table sat five figures dressed in the same manner as him.

Five pairs of eyes watched through the narrow slits of the hoods as Benedict entered the room. He bowed once, made the sign of the cross, and took his place at the table. No one spoke. He lifted his eyes to the large tapestry or arras that covered the wall opposite. It depicted an army of mounted knights charging into battle across a frozen landscape. They wore black tunics over their armour with the white cross of the Order. Their visors were raised to reveal their features – though in reality, as Benedict knew, they would have been closed for battle – and one of them, riding near the centre, bore a remarkable likeness to himself, though as the date of the battle was 1346 most observers would have taken this for coincidence.

After a few minutes, the door opened again and another figure entered the room, robed and hooded like the others but with a distinctive symbol beneath the cross. It showed an angel in a golden circle with a sword held before him and radiating from the blade were seven golden beams of light. The insignia of the Knight Commander.

The newcomer took the last seat at the table and extended his hands, palms uppermost, to those seated on each side of him and they in turn to their neighbours so that all seven were joined by the hands. Then the Knight Commander led them in saying the Lord's Prayer. At the concluding Amen, all seven members of the Order threw back their hoods. Benedict appeared to be the youngest by several decades.

'The Military Council of the Knights of the Order of Saint Saviour of Antioch is now in session,' announced the Knight Commander. 'I would remind everyone present that these discussions are secret. They cannot be shared with anyone, not even members of the Order, or in the privacy of the confessional. And there will no minutes taken.'

Then, in a less formal tone, he continued: 'Welcome, brothers. Thank you for coming to Rome at short notice to attend this Extraordinary General Meeting. I know some of you have had to travel a considerable distance to do so. However, I am afraid it has been forced upon us by certain developments concerning the case of Brother Boris.'

A collective shudder passed around the table. Clearly this was not the first time they had heard the name.

'You are all aware, I am sure, of the general background to the case,' the Knight Commander continued. 'However, for the purposes of this meeting may I remind you of the relevant circumstances?'

He paused for a moment to gather his thoughts.

'Brother Boris is, as are many of our Order, a doctor of medicine. He is also a scientist who has been engaged for many years in the study of genetics. Indeed he worked for a time as Professor of Genetics at the university here in Rome. However, certain of his studies – and other activities – were condemned by the papal authorities. When he persisted with them he was expelled from the Order and excommunicated from the Church. However, he continued to practise as a scientist in England, using the name Kobal.'

He glanced briefly toward Brother Benedict as if for confirmation of this fact but the younger monk said nothing and his face remained impassive.

'The British government was reluctant to release full details of the case but from our own inquiries it appears he was engaged in the study of inherited diseases. It soon became clear, however, that he had far exceeded the boundaries of this brief and that he was involved in an attempt to, as it were, improve the species. To produce a more perfect form of human being. In fact one might say, the first of a new breed of super-humans.'

Another murmur ran around the table and one voice was raised in anger:

'Playing God.'

'Or the Devil,' said another. All eyes turned to him. He was a venerable old man, the oldest of those present, with a face like a skull, save for the wispy white beard that covered the lower part of it, and the eyes that stared out of the dark sockets were bright with passion, or a kind of fever. 'The Devil,' he repeated, in a strong, ringing voice that belied his years, looking around the table as if challenging any to contradict him. 'You must all know it, or have suspected it. For certainly he is about the Devil's work.'

'Brothers.' The Knight Commander raised a hand. 'Let us not be diverted into a discussion of the moral issues. The simple fact is that Brother Boris – Dr Kobal – or whatever he cares to call himself – broke the law, and not only in the United Kingdom. He indulged in experiments that are banned by international law. He was convicted of a number of related crimes and committed to a hospital for the criminally insane.'

'Insane!' The old monk's voice was mocking, as if this was a ridiculous notion, a flawed concept of the modern world.

'Are you saying he isn't?' cried another.

'Brothers.' Once more the Knight Commander raised his hand. 'If we are to embark on a debate into whether Brother Boris is, or isn't, insane we will be here all night, and possibly all eternity. It was the judgment of the English courts, which is all that need concern us here. However – incredible as it may seem – he was permitted to continue certain of his researches whilst in prison. Indeed, a laboratory was provided for him in the prison grounds. And –' he raised his voice above the tide of amazed and indignant protests '– and in the course of time, he contrived to escape. Taking with him a number of human embryos—'

'Dear God!'

'Outrageous!'

'The Devil! The Devil's work!'

The Knight Commander continued though he was now almost shouting to be heard. 'Human embryos that were planted in the wombs of seven surrogate mothers who, in due course, gave birth to seven children . . . Brothers, please, may I have your attention for there is more.' He sighed wearily. 'Much more.'

Brother Benedict raised a hand.

'On a point of information, Knight Commander, we have only been able to account for six children.'

'I beg your pardon, Brother. Six children. And one unaccounted for.' He paused. 'I think, Brother, you had best tell the rest of the story as you are acquainted with the facts at first hand.'

Benedict nodded and gazed at the frowning faces around the table.

'Dr Kobal was on the run,' he said. 'There was a warrant out for his arrest. The mothers – I should say the *host* mothers – returned to their homes in various parts of the world with the seven children. Here they remained for seven years. Kobal's whereabouts in that time remained a mystery. However, it became known to us, through our network of agents, that he was making an effort to recover his lost family and bring them to a refuge he had established in the far north of Finland. A place known to the locals as Castle Piru, the Castle of Demons.'

A snort of triumph from the oldest monk.

'What did I tell you?'

Benedict made no comment. 'For reasons that are unclear to us, it took several years for Kobal to locate the children. But by the early spring of this year, he had managed to find six of them and bring them to

Castle Piru. We believe he was still looking for the seventh child. But his other activities – certain experiments he was making on the local wildlife –' growls of anger and horror from his audience '– aroused the suspicions of the local people, who decided to take the law into their own hands. They attacked the castle and it was burned to the ground. Kobal, however, escaped into Russia, taking most of the children with him. All but one.'

'All but one?'

'Yes. One of the children managed to escape – with our assistance. A young girl. She was returned to her home in England and is now in a Catholic boarding school for girls, run by one of the Holy Orders.'

A grunt of approval.

'And the others?'

'Unfortunately we have no news of them.'

A brooding silence, broken at length by the Knight Commander.

'Brothers, we have very little authority in this matter. Indeed, no official powers whatsoever. However Dr Kobal is, to some extent, our responsibility. A renegade. And the Holy Father has personally expressed his concern in this matter.

We are doing everything we can to find him – with the assistance of the secular authorities where it is forthcoming.'

'And if we do?'

'He will be returned to the custody of the British authorities – and they, I assume, will return him to Houndwood Hospital for the criminally insane.'

'Ha!' snorted the ancient. 'The fiend must be returned to Hell. If he is not there already.'

'And the children?'

'They too.'

'Please.' The Knight Commander's voice was sharp. 'Brother Alois, let us remember which century we are living in. The children will be returned to their homes, wherever possible. Or taken into care. That, again, is the responsibility of the secular authorities.'

One of the brothers turned toward Benedict.

'Are they normal?'

'What do you mean by normal?'

'I think you know what I mean, Brother Benedict. They have been tampered with – "improved" – or, I believe one might say, "genetically modified". As if they were grains of wheat or barley. What form does this "modification" take?'

'It takes a variety of forms. Increased intelligence,

perception — certain physical and mental abilities . . .'

'Such as?'

'They are not monsters, Brother Franz.' Benedict's voice was soft but his eyes were like chips of ice. 'They are children. Children of exceptional ability in some cases — but children nonetheless and deserving of our protection.'

'Brothers, brothers.' The Knight Commander raised his arms once more. 'Let us not quarrel over matters of which we have little or no understanding at present. The important thing is to find them — and to find the man who has committed these . . . atrocities, and put him back in a place where he can do no further harm. The purpose of this meeting was to inform you of the circumstances and to seek your assistance in tracking the man down — under Brother Benedict's overall command. Do I have your assent to that?'

Nods from around the table, grudging in some cases.

'Then the decision is unanimous,' said the Knight Commander. 'Before I declare the meeting closed is there any other business relating to this issue?' He raised his bushy brows as if daring anyone to take up the invitation.

'I would like to ask Brother Benedict one more thing,' said Brother Alois.

The Knight Commander sighed resignedly. 'Very well.'

'Why do you think he chose to have *seven* children?'

'You know as well as we that it has always been regarded as a mystic number,' the Knight Commander protested. 'That is why *we* are seven.'

'I asked Brother Benedict,' the old man insisted.

'Well, the Septagram has always been a kind of talisman for him,' Benedict explained. 'The seven-pointed star, or the magic star, as some call it. Each point has a name . . .' He ticked them off on his fingers. 'Forest, Fire, Water, Wind, Moon, Magic, Spirit. And each of the children seems to be linked with one of these points in some way.'

'In what way?'

Benedict shot the Knight Commander a glance, but receiving no sign he replied: 'Either because they were born there – in the place of Fire or Water or whatever – or sent there shortly after they were born.'

'But for what reason?'

'We don't know,' said Brother Benedict. 'It is a mystery.'

★　★　★

Benedict walked back alone across the Ponte Sant'Angelo, his brow creased in thought. Sheets of rain drifted through the floodlights that illuminated the great fortress but he seemed as heedless of it as the stone angels lining the bridge. Nor did he notice the two men watching him from the barred window high above the castle gatehouse, and if he had, he probably would have made little of it, despite their appearance.

One wore the ceremonial robes of the Order of Knights, the tall cowl almost hiding his features. The other wore a smart black overcoat and a hat known as a fedora, its wide brim bent low over the eyes. Much favoured by 1920s gangsters and private detectives, it was enjoying something of a revival among men of fashion and this was the real thing, made by the original manufacturer, Borsalino, in Piedmont, though his venerable companion was ignorant of such niceties.

'There he goes,' he said, his eyes glinting fiercely as he stared down at the distant figure crossing the bridge. 'There's your man.'

'And what do you want done with him?' The voice was bored, as if the speaker was indifferent to the answer.

'I just want him followed, for the moment,' replied the monk. 'I want to know exactly where he goes and who he sees. But you should have sufficient men available to do whatever is necessary – should it be required.'

'How many do you think it requires,' enquired his companion, in a tone of contempt, looking down at the solitary figure on the bridge, 'to deal with one man?'

'Do not underestimate him,' snapped the monk. 'He is extremely dangerous and . . . it is not for him alone.'

'So how many are there?'

'Apart from him – seven. And the men you choose should not be at all squeamish.'

'*Squeamish?*' The man laughed.

'I know. I know. But let me put it this way – you should not choose anyone who is, let us say, at all sentimental where children are concerned.'

The man looked at him sharply. 'I see,' he said, and then more thoughtfully, 'I see.'

'Is that a problem for you?'

'No . . . not personally but . . . yes, you are right, I will have to choose my people with some care. Italians are often "sentimental" where children are concerned. And the price, of course, will have to reflect that.'

'It will,' the monk acknowledged with a sigh. He looked back towards the man on the bridge and frowned. 'What is he doing?'

The object of his enquiry had stopped halfway across the bridge. He was peering over the parapet as if he had seen something in the water. Then suddenly he looked up towards the castle – so sharply and directly that the two men instinctively stepped back into the shadows though there was little chance of their being seen. Then he began to run swiftly in the opposite direction until he was lost in the darkness.

'What was all that about?' queried the monk in a troubled voice.

'I don't know,' said his companion with a shrug. 'But I'd better get my people on to it. Before we lose him.'

8

Trapped

It was like the start of her nightmare, only worse. Certainly there had been a descent, though not for long. And now there was darkness, total darkness, the darkness of the abyss. Jade's groping hands encountered something solid, unyielding, above her head and though she pressed against it with all her strength she could not move it: she could not break free from the nightmare.

Then, as some kind of feeling returned to her numbed senses, the full horror of her situation exploded into her consciousness. It was not a nightmare. This was real. She was in a car — what she could feel was the roof — and the reason it was so dark was because they were at the bottom of a river.

Then the panic came. She felt for the door handle but there was something pinning her back, pressing against her chest. The seatbelt. She found the release and the pressure eased, though she felt as if someone had punched her in the chest.

Then she remembered Aunt Em.

She reached towards her in the darkness and her fingers touched something warm – and soft – and wet.

'Aunt Em! Aunt Em!'

Her hands felt a sticky substance that she knew must be blood. She began to cry then because she knew her guardian must be dead, or terribly injured.

'No!'

The shout echoed in Jade's ears, as if she was in a drum, but it did not come from her.

'No, no, no, no!' yelled Emily and then she was like a wild thing, a trapped animal, lashing out with her arms.

'Aunt Em, Aunt Em!'

'Jade?'

'It's all right, it's all right,' said Jade, even though the one thing it wasn't was all right. 'I'm here.'

'What happened? Where am I?'

'We had a crash. We're in the car.'

'I can't see. Oh God, I've gone blind.'

'No, you're not blind. It's dark.'

'Oh, thank God for that!' Emily sobbed with relief.

Jade gave her the bad news. 'We're in the river.'

'Oh God, oh God! We're in the river!'

But Jade was thinking more calmly now. It was only a river. It wasn't the sea. It couldn't be deep. If they could only open the door . . . She groped for the handle again in the dark and pressed it down, leaning her shoulder against the door. But it wouldn't budge.

She heard her guardian's voice, calmer now.

'Jade, are you all right?'

'Yeah. I'm fine.'

'What are you doing?'

'Trying to open the door.'

'Are you mad? Jade – we're in a river.'

'But we've got to get out.'

'You can't open the door.'

'Why not?'

'Because of the pressure of the water. Let me think . . . My God, I'm bleeding.'

'I know. I felt it.'

'It's all right. I think it's only a nose bleed.'

'Oh, I thought it was your brain.'

'What?'

'I thought it was your brain leaking out of your head.'

'It must have been the airbag. My God! It's coming through the floor.'

'What is?'

'Water.'

'Yeah, well, we're in a river,' Jade pointed out. 'It would.'

Then she began to sneeze.

'Achooo! Achooo!'

'OK, OK, listen to me. We've got to think carefully about this.'

'Achooo! I can't stop snee— Achooo!'

'It's the talcum powder.'

'*What?*'

'From the airbag. They use it as a lubricant. Hold your nose and listen to me. You've got to do exactly what I say.'

'Achooo! All right. Whab do you wan me to do?'

'I don't suppose the electrics work but just try the window on your side, will you?'

Jade stopped holding her nose.

'Excuse me? You've just told me not to open the door, now you want me to open the window.'

'Just try it. Please.'

Jade did. It didn't work. But at least she'd stopped sneezing.

'OK. Just see if my handbag's at your feet.'

'Your handbag? What do you want with your handbag?'

'Just pass it to me, will you?'

A moment later the interior of the car was filled with light. Emily pointed a small torch down towards the floor. It reflected black water. But not much – considering they were in a river.

'It'll take for ever,' she said. She balanced the torch on the dash so it reflected back from the roof, filling the car with an eerie light. Then she bent down to unzip her boots.

'Why are you taking off your boots?' Jade asked her.

'Because they're Pradas, my darling, and I don't want to get them wet.'

Jade stared at her, wondering if it was the knock on the head. Now she was climbing over the seat with one of the boots in her hand.

'Now what are you doing?'

'I'm going to try to smash the back window.'

It suddenly dawned on Jade. 'You want us to die quicker.'

Emily stopped in mid-climb and looked seriously at her.

'Jade, we're not going to die. OK?'

'OK.' Jade's teeth were chattering and her whole body was shivering uncontrollably. So they weren't going to die.

'Now, listen. The doors won't open because the pressure of the water outside is greater than the pressure of the air inside. So we need to let the water in. But before it fills the car completely, you have to take a deep breath and then open the door and get out as fast as you can. OK?'

'OK but . . .'

But Emily was already smashing the heel of her boot into the window and, after several violent blows, it exploded inwards bringing a significant portion of the river with it. She climbed back into the front seat. She looked very wet.

'Now, whatever you do, don't panic,' she said. 'Wait until the water's up to your neck, then take a deep breath and open the door. OK?'

'OK.' Jade thought of something. 'And what are *you* going to do?'

'Oh, I'm just going to sit here and see if I can get Jazz FM on the radio.'

'I was only asking.'

'You're a good girl,' said Emily. 'A good, brave girl.' She felt for Jade's hand in the darkness. 'I love you, babe.'

It was almost worth being trapped in a car at the bottom of a river just to hear her say that.

The water was rising fast. It was already up to Jade's waist. She took a deep breath and tried the door. It still wouldn't open. She felt the panic rising with the water and fought it. But the water was so cold, it took her breath away. She was breathing in short, panic-stricken gasps as the water rose to her chest. She felt for the door again and it still wouldn't open. She began to whimper – but then suddenly there seemed to be a kind of light all around her and she could hear a voice that seemed to be coming from inside her head.

Take a deep breath. Now let it out. Slowly. As if you were snorkelling.

As if she was snorkelling. She had never been snorkelling but somehow she knew what the voice meant.

She took another deep breath. The water was

almost up to her neck but she felt completely calm, almost relaxed. And she was no longer cold. She tried the door again and this time it opened. She felt the water close over her head. But she was all right with that now. Slowly and deliberately she moved out of her seat and out of the car and into the river.

9

The Terrible River

There are few things worse than being trapped in a car at the bottom of a river but, as Jade soon discovered, the surface of the river is not all that comfortable either, especially when it is in flood.

She exploded into a world of sound and storm and furious swirling water – and an intense biting cold, a cold that seemed to make the inside of the car at the bottom of a river seem almost cosy.

And a blazing light that hit her right in the face, dazzling her.

The light was a surprise. She had not expected the light. It was a flashlight, she realized in the brief moment before other concerns wiped it from her mind: a flashlight sweeping the surface of the water.

She did not see the figure, or figures, behind it but she knew they must be from the other car. Barmella, perhaps, or even Kobal himself. This was not something she was allowed to dwell upon, for the river was in flood, a raging torrent fed by a thousand lesser torrents, swollen by rainwater pouring off the surrounding hills. It had burst its banks, rising almost to the arch of the bridge and sweeping all before it: branches, lengths of fencing, sheds, dead sheep, flotsam and jetsam of every description – and Jade.

She was swept away at a rate of knots, leaving the flashlight, the car, the bridge far behind her: a blur of images engraved on her mind before the darkness swallowed them up and she was fighting for her life.

She was a good swimmer. In a swimming pool. This was different. You couldn't swim in this. You certainly couldn't swim *against* it. You were just one more piece of debris caught up in the flood. You just went with the flow and tried to keep your head above the water.

And oh, it was cold. So cold she wanted to give up, to surrender to it, to sink into the illusory warmth of death.

And where was Aunt Em? Was she dead already, or fighting for her own life just a few metres away? Jade called out to her but there was no answering cry from the darkness.

Something crashed into her, knocking what little breath she had left in her body but somehow she managed to cling to it. A tree, or a large branch. She pulled herself a little out of the water and searched for another bobbing head but it was impossible to see anything in that relentless surge. It was like a great black-backed beast, a wild thing, a monstrous serpent surging through the night. And so cold. Deathly cold. One shivering misery of cold. If she let go she would sink and it would all be over. There was a warm fire waiting for her . . . Only let go.

No, another voice commanded sternly. *Don't even think about it.*

A great crash. Her life-raft had hit one of the trees that lined the banks, the former banks, now deep in water. Another crash and she screamed and almost lost her grip. It was a bend in the river. And the bank was high at this point, a rocky crag, a cliff almost, with a cluster of trees at its foot and the rushing waters surging around them. Crash! Another tree. And this time she lost her precious hold. The waters closed over her. She surfaced, gasping and choking, and went down again, down for the last time . . . except that her groping fingers found a trailing root or branch and held on, knowing it was her last chance of life, the river pulling at her like a live thing . . . And she was swept round like a limp rag and dumped into a backwater in the lee of a rocky outcrop, a miraculous haven from the monster's fury.

She dragged herself up on to the slippery surface of the rock. Rain and spray lashed her face and the river surged at her feet, threatening to hurl her back into its clutches. But there was a tree rising above her, sticking out from the very base of the cliff, just clear of the flood water . . . She took a few tottering steps and clung to it. At last she felt safe from the river, but she could not stay here. She was shivering uncontrollably with cold and shock. Unless she found shelter and warmth she would die. She looked up at the cliff above. Impossible. But she had to try. She forced herself to concentrate, to look for some means of climbing that towering cliff. And yet it wasn't so very high – no more than thirty or forty metres perhaps – and there were more trees growing out from the side, out over the river, their roots clinging to the soil and rock, the trunks projecting outwards at an angle.

She began to drag herself up by root and branch,

87

her feet sliding from under her on the slippery slope, stones and muck dropping into the river below, rain and mud sluicing down on her. Several times she slid back but managed to grab a hold before she plunged to her death – for she would die, she knew, if she fell into that river again. It was like some deadly game of snakes and ladders. But she was so tired. She had to rest. She made it to the next tree, the last tree, the river below like a pit filled with angry writhing serpents hissing and roaring for her, their vanished prey, almost hypnotizing her to let go and drop back into their greedy jaws. She looked up. She could see the top of the cliff now just three or four metres above her head. But they were three or four metres of sheer rock, slick with rain. There were no more trees, no more ladders . . .

She could not have come so far only to be cheated now. She stood up with her back against the tree feeling the rain on her face, the rain and the tears.

And then she saw the bough.

It was just above her head, growing at a sharp angle towards the top of the cliff.

She turned very carefully, shuffling her feet round one after the other until she was facing the tree. Her cheek was pressed against the wet bark, her arms wrapped around the trunk as if she was hugging it. She groped around in the darkness for a handhold. Nothing. But then as she stretched her hands up as far as she could on either side of the tree, she found something. A knobbly knot of wood, a little above her head. Not much of a hold but enough, if she had the strength – and the courage. She clawed her fingers into the wood and heaved, pulling herself bit by bit up the greasy pole, reaching with her left hand for the branch just a few tantalizing centimetres higher. If she slipped now nothing would save her. But then her fingers closed round the precious lifeline and she hung on with her left hand, almost pulling her shoulder out at the socket, and made a grab with the right. Now she was hanging from the bough with both arms. All she had to do was pull herself up. Barmella had made her do chin-ups often enough in the gym in the Castle of Demons. She could still hear that fiendish voice driving her on.

Von more, only von. Von more. You can do it!

She'd managed twelve at the last count.

She heaved, scrabbling with her feet against the tree trunk until she was hanging upside down like a sloth. One more effort. *Just von more.* She managed to throw one leg over, then an arm. Now her whole body. Yes! Panting with exhaustion, lying full length along the branch. Less like a slimy sloth now, more like a leopard.

Thank you, Barmella. Did you know that all those workouts were for this – so I could escape from you?

But now what?

She knew now what. She had to crawl up that sloping, slender limb towards the top of the ridge. With nothing beneath her but the river and the rocks.

But she couldn't. She wasn't a leopard. Or even a sloth.

There were only two ways of doing this. She either had to sit astride it and shuffle along on her bottom – or she had to stand up and walk along it.

She knew that was the best way but she dreaded it. She wasn't an acrobat either.

She eased herself up so she was standing with her back against the trunk and the branch arching away towards the top of the cliff. She could just see the clumps of grass at the edge. And beyond to the open countryside and the dark humps of the sleeping fells in the distance, darker even than the sky. Not a light, no sign of shelter, as far as she could see.

But she would worry about that later. She reached

out a foot, still supporting herself with one hand against the tree trunk.

But she couldn't do it. Not like this she couldn't. She had to take a run at it. Two steps and a jump.

She froze with horror at the thought. She was shivering again, her whole body wracked with shuddering sobs and her teeth like piano keys beating a frantic tuneless dirge, a funeral dirge. She forced herself to be still, conjured up an image of herself soaring through the air to safety.

OK, let's do it!

One, two . . . and a great scream as her foot slipped.

Down she plunged into the abyss. But her momentum hurled her against the face of the cliff and she threw out a hand and grabbed hold of the grass growing along the top. A thick clump of grass in each hand, like the hair on a giant's head.

And slowly, ever so slowly, she pulled herself up until she was lying on solid ground.

It was only then that she remembered it was her father's favourite expression: *Let's do it*.

And then she looked up and saw the hooded figure staring down at her and heard the familiar mocking voice.

'Well done. Once or twice there, I thought you

weren't going to make it and I'd have to send Baer-Mellor down after you.'

The voice of her father. Kobal.

10

The Seven Trumpets

Black rags of cloud raced across the moon like fleeing spectres, tinged with an eerie light. The vicious wind howled across the ravaged earth, driving the rain before it, a merciless hail flaying the bare backs of the crouching fells. And from the storm-tossed branches of the beech trees surrounding the old rectory a colony of crows gazed down upon the three human figures approaching from the direction of the river and clicked their beaks like disapproving curates.

In fact Jade was barely recognizable as human. Her wet clothing clung to her body, she was plastered with mud, blood leaked from a score of scratches, her face was deathly white, and she was shivering uncontrollably. She looked like one of the Undead that had so terrified her roommates at Saint Severa's.

The woman she knew as Barmella finally scooped her up and carried her the rest of the way, opening the door by the simple method of kicking it in and heading straight up the stairs to the bathroom. Jade was barely conscious of having her wet clothes stripped off her and being lifted into a bath full of steaming hot water. She put her head back and closed her eyes and let the warmth and the weariness sweep over.

'No, you do not sleep.'

Barmella revived her by the simple method of turning the shower head on her and spraying her with cold water. Jade gasped but it was no use complaining or appealing for sympathy. It would be like trying to melt a block of ice with frozen tears.

When she was little, Jade had possessed a doll that she called Barmella. She had treated it very badly, throwing it against the wall and even burying it in the garden once in a mock funeral. She had no idea where the name came from and indeed it had puzzled her foster parents at the time. 'Why Barmella?' they had said and Jade could only shake her head and say, 'Because it is.' Then, years later, she had met the Countess Sophie Baer-Mellor von

Koffen and realized it had been some weird kind of presentiment. It wasn't just that they looked the same, with the same over-large hands and head, the same cold blue eyes, the absence of hair — the doll's had fallen out but the Countess probably shaved. But they shared the same indifference to pain and suffering. Their own and anyone else's. It was as if the Countess Baer-Mellor was the doll Barmella come to life, to exact some kind of grim revenge. To throw her against walls and perhaps even bury her, whenever her father gave the word.

This time Barmella just threw her a bar of soap and told her to wash. Jade washed. It was only then that she noticed all the cuts and bruises. And of course they immediately started to hurt. She thought briefly of mentioning this to Barmella — but only briefly.

'Now out,' said Barmella. She threw her a towel. 'Dry.'

Jade dried and Barmella indicated a pile of clothes draped over a chair.

'Dress,' she said.

Jade had begun to shiver again and she didn't need any urging, even though they weren't the kind of clothes she might have chosen for herself. There was thermal underwear, a sweater several sizes too big for her and a pair of baggy jeans and thick woollen socks.

'Come,' said Barmella.

Jade followed her downstairs and into the living room and there, sitting toasting his feet beside a roaring log fire, was her father. The man she thought of as Kobal. Or the Devil.

'Well, well, well, my little Child of the Forest.'

He had grown a beard since they last met. Not much of one, more like designer stubble. It made him look even more like Johnny Depp in *Pirates of the Caribbean*, a resemblance that Jade had noted and which she believed he encouraged. His long dark hair was hanging loose – sometimes he tied it in a pony tail – and he wore a ring in one ear. Sometimes he used kohl on his eyes, but not now, probably because of the rain. He looked about thirty at the most and he spoke in the posh English voice he sometimes used when he was talking to Jade, presumably in mockery because she had been brought up in England and he seemed to find this amusing. His normal accent – if there was anything remotely approaching normal about Kobal – was American English and he claimed to be from New York, though this was almost certainly a lie, like most of the things he told you. Where he really came from was a mystery, at least to Jade. She wondered where he had been hiding since she had last seen him. Given that he was on the run from half the police forces in the world it had to be somewhere remote.

'I'll do a deal with you,' said Jade with a pretence at calm. 'I'll come quietly if you phone the police and tell them you saw a car go into the river.'

He stared at her in mock amazement.

'But why on earth should I do that?'

'Because Aunt Em's out there and she'll be freezing to death.'

Jade felt sure she had managed to get out of the car. She had been so calm and collected and she was a good swimmer; she had taught Jade how to swim when she was little.

'Please,' she implored him. 'She'll die if we don't get help.'

'Aunt Em?' Kobal frowned at Barmella. 'Do we know this person?'

'Dr Mortlake,' said Barmella.

But he knew very well who Jade meant. 'Ah, Dr Mortlake. My former colleague. The traitor. The informer.' He considered Jade carefully. Despite her attempt at control she felt her eyes fill with tears. 'Oh, very well,' he shrugged. 'Countess, phone the police. Tell them you saw a car in the river. And while you're about it, see if you can root out a decent bottle of wine from the cellar.'

'A vine cellar? In this place?' Barmella had a problem with Kobal's sense of humour. Or anyone else's for that matter.

'Well, wherever they keep the old vino, then. I don't suppose it will be up to our usual standard but I feel we deserve a drink after a night like tonight.'

'Please!' Jade implored him.

'Oh, all right, all right.' He fluttered his fingers dismissively at Barmella. 'Do as the child wishes or we'll never get any peace.'

Jade sank down on her knees.

'You're not going to pray, are you?' he demanded archly. 'Because I really don't think I could cope. It's bad enough being in a vicarage.'

'A vicarage?' She gazed around her wonderingly. 'What are you doing in a vicarage?'

He could not possibly have become a vicar. Though she wouldn't put anything past Kobal.

'Or a rectory,' he mused. 'I think that's the right word. Baer–Mellor found it on the internet. It's a holiday home. The Church sold most of their old rectories years ago. Moved the staff into bungalows. Quite right, too.'

He could go on like this for hours, following a strand of thought. Sometimes Jade thought it was deliberate, so you could never pin him down.

'How long have you been here?'

'Oh, not long. Now that we've found you. I expect you've missed me,' he added with a beam.

She looked at him scathingly as he toasted his stockinged feet at the fire. He always said he felt the cold, even though he chose to live in the far north of Finland – probably because that was the only place he felt safe from the police. He was taking a real chance coming back to England – though she didn't think for a minute that he'd come through customs and immigration like any normal person. He'd probably flown into some remote airport in a private jet.

'So where are the rest of them?' she demanded coldly.

'*The rest of them?*' He looked about the room as if people were hiding there.

'The kids. My so-called brothers and sisters?'

'Half-brothers and -sisters. As I have told you on more than one occasion. They all had different mothers.'

'Whatever.'

'They're very well, thank you. They all send their love. Little Paco in particular.'

'Ha.'

He knew very well what she thought of 'little Paco'. He was a monster. The worst of a bad bunch in Jade's opinion. She'd found him on a rubbish dump in Guatemala City, where their loving father had left him for most of his life. But he'd turned out to be such a little thug she wished they'd left him there. She didn't really like any of them but then she hardly knew them. They'd been born and raised in different parts of the world by different mothers, or foster parents, or orphanages. Or left to fend for themselves like Paco. And now, for some reason, Kobal wanted them to be together.

'So where are they?' she demanded. 'Have you got them in the back of the car?'

'No, alas. I was forced to leave them in a safe place, owing to the rather unfortunate circumstances in which you left us.'

With an army of reindeer herders trying to burn them to death. She was lucky to have survived herself.

Barmella came in with two bottles and several glasses gathered together in her large hands.

'Vine no good,' she said. 'But here is visky. Scotch visky.' She showed Kobal the bottles. He examined the labels with interest.

'Did you phone the police?' Jade demanded. 'What did they say?'

'They say they send someone to look,' Barmella informed her coldly. But without meeting her eyes.

'They need a helicopter,' Jade insisted. 'They need the mountain rescue.'

'That is so. That is what they say. They send the mountain rescue.'

Jade wondered if she could believe her. She looked despairingly towards the window as it rattled in the wind. It didn't seem possible that Aunt Em could be dead. But she was flesh and blood like any normal person; she could hurt, she could bleed. She could die. She might be out there on the fells, freezing to death.

'A Bladnoch!' Kobal exclaimed. 'Fifteen years old. This is a very good single malt.' He held it up for them to see. 'Established in 1817 by Thomas McClelland in Dumfries. Outstanding.' He frowned. 'Where on earth did you find one of these?'

'In the kitchen.'

'In the kitchen? I don't believe it.' He gazed at the

label again in astonishment. 'They must have known I was coming.'

'Do you want I get you some vater?'

'Water? With a Bladnoch! You're kidding me. Same for you?' he enquired of Jade. 'It's a Bladnoch.'

So Jade had gathered.

'She does not drink the alcohol,' Barmella reminded him. 'She is a young girl. I bring you juice,' she informed Jade imperiously.

'Ah, ambrosia! Liquid fire!' Kobal sampled the whisky and closed his eyes in ecstasy. Then he opened them and surveyed Jade amiably. 'Now then, tell us what you've been up to since we last saw you.'

'You know very well what I've been up to,' Jade told him crossly. 'You sent *her* to spy on me.'

'Oh, I wouldn't say that. Spy on you indeed. I sent her to scout out the location in the guise of a prospective parent so we could come and rescue you. As you so clearly needed rescuing. Convent school indeed. I bet I know who thought of that. However, we'll soon have you back in the bosom of the family and we can continue with your proper education.'

'And where will that be? Seeing as they burned you out of the last place. And you're wanted by almost every police force in the world.'

He frowned. 'Things have been a little difficult lately,' he conceded. 'No small thanks to you, or those of your acquaintance who appear determined to thwart my designs. However, once I have you all together, all seven of you . . .'

He regarded her carefully and she knew he was trying to read her mind. Not that he had to try very hard. Most of the time he could read her like an open book. She flushed.

'You haven't found him yet, have you?'

'Found who?'

'Number seven.'

A slight change of expression, a narrowing of the eyes as if he was contemplating whether this was an impertinence, meriting punishment.

'No. Not yet. But I've had other things on my mind, thanks to you and your interfering friends. Won't be long now, though. Now I can focus on the problem and I have you to assist me.' He raised his hand up to his mouth. 'Come in, Number Seven,' he called out, as if he were hiring boats on a park lake, 'your time is up.' Then he put on a different voice. 'Come out, come out, wherever you are.' Like the voice of Jack Nicholson in *The Shining*. He fancied himself as a bit of a mimic and he was a complete freak for the movies. He bared his teeth in a horrible Jack Nicholas grin, his eyes totally mad. 'Here's Johnny!'

Jade shuddered. 'Why can't you leave him alone? He obviously doesn't want to be found. Not by you.'

'Oh, but we have to find him. He's our missing link. Our Child of the Spirit. Our little Romanian gypsy boy.'

He had pet names for all of them, based on what he called the Septagram — his magic star. It had something to do with the places they'd been born, though Jade didn't understand it completely. She didn't understand much that came from the mind of her father. She was the Child of the Forest. Born in the Forest of Windsor, in a hospital prison for the criminally insane, where he'd been staying at the time, as a guest of Her Majesty's Government.

'Romanian?' she said.

He smiled at her.

'So he's from Romania?' she repeated.

'Oh, well done.' He gave her the thumbs-up. 'Great school they sent you to, there. Yes. Romania. The land of Dracula.'

She flushed again, wondering if he knew all about her games at Saint Severa's. It was likely.

'Dracula. And gypsies. And orphans. Poor little orphans, like our Child of the Spirit, looking for a home.'

'Why don't you leave him in peace?' Jade demanded, losing her temper; he looked so infuriatingly smug, holding the glass so he could admire the amber liquid in the light of the fire. 'What do you want with him? What do you want with any of us?'

'You know what I want with you. Together we are going to save the planet.'

'You're mad,' she said again. 'Totally barking. They ought to lock you up.'

'You think *I'm* mad? Have you looked at the world lately?'

'OK, if you think you can do something about it go ahead, but leave me out of it. I've got my own life to live.'

'Oh, yes – and was it so wonderful before I found you? Did you have any purpose in life? Look at you. No one wants you. As soon as they got you back they sent you away again – to a wretched little convent school in the middle of nowhere. Outrageous! I didn't raise you to become a nun.'

'You didn't raise me,' she snapped angrily. 'I didn't

see you for ten years. Not that I'm complaining. I wish I'd never seen you.'

'Doing all right without me then, are you? People looking after you all right? Dear me. My eldest daughter a nun.'

'You don't go there to become a nun. You go there to be educated.'

He did a double take. 'Educated? For what? For what kind of *life* were they educating you? For what kind of *world* were they preparing you?'

She shrugged. 'Dunno,' she said. She knew this would annoy him.

'*Dunno. You don't know?* No, you don't know, my girl. Do they teach you to adapt, to survive, to cope with the destruction of the environment, the ruin of the forests, the pollution of the seas, the thawing of the icecaps? No, the summit of your ambition is to be a celebrity on some television show – or marry a footballer.'

'Actually they're not so keen on that at Saint Severa's,' Jade pointed out, but she was wasting her time. He wasn't listening. He was off on one of his rants.

'The world is racing to destruction and what do you do, you mindless children of the Apocalypse?

You carry on just as before. Consuming the world's resources as if there is no tomorrow. Can you not heed the signs? Can you not hear the blast of the trumpets?'

Jade pretended to listen. 'I think that's the wind,' she said.

That got through to him all right. 'You think this is funny?' he asked with a dangerous glint in his eye. 'You think it's all a big laugh? I don't think so. I don't think there's going to be much laughter when the seven trumpets sound.'

'What seven trumpets?'

'The trumpets that herald the Final Days of Man. The Apocalypse. The beginning of the Age of Abaddon.' He began to quote. ' "*And when the fifth trumpet sounds a star will fall to earth and open the Abyss. And out of the bottomless pit will come locusts like horses arrayed for battle. And they shall have as king over them the Angel of the Abyss whose name is Abaddon.*" '

At last there was silence – apart from the wind and the rain . . . And something else, something vaguely familiar.

'What's that?' he said, sitting up straight and alert. 'Switch off the light,' he instructed Barmella and all three ran to the window and pushed back the curtain

– and there it was in the night sky, like a great fat locust with one eye glaring down.

A helicopter.

11

The Road Block

They watched from the window as the helicopter hovered above the river, its searchlight probing the rushing flood waters below. Kobal and Barmella exchanged glances.

'I guess we should be moving on,' said Kobal.

'You'll never get away with it,' Jade insisted. 'They'll have roadblocks. They'll have people at the airports and everything.'

Kobal ignored her. 'Let's take a look at the map,' he instructed Barmella. They unfolded it on the table.

'They'll have my description,' Jade persisted. 'They'll be looking for a man and woman with a girl my age. You might as well leave me here.'

But of course, he wasn't worried who was looking

for them. He could make people think whatever he wanted them to think, see what he wanted them to see. He could make them think he was royalty if he wanted to. They'd probably lay on an escort to the nearest airport.

She didn't understand how he did it. Sometimes she thought he *was* the Devil. Other times that he was just a clever trickster who had learned some form of mind control, like a kind of hypnotism. Impressive but not superhuman. And even though he hated to admit it, there were limits to his powers. He couldn't control everybody. He couldn't rule the world, or even a small part of it, much as he'd like to. He wouldn't want a scene – and Jade was very good at making a scene, just give her half a chance.

She tried to catch a glimpse of the map. Barmella was trailing her finger in the direction of the Lake District. Of course. A seaplane. Kobal had a thing about seaplanes. They were his favourite toys and they didn't have to land at airports. Any decent stretch of water would do. What was the nearest lake to here? She reviewed her own mental map. Ullswater. About twelve miles west of Appleby. They could be there in half an hour.

'Right,' said Kobal decisively. 'We'll be on our way.'

But Barmella had more clothes for her. A Goretex survival suit with a hood. A pair of waterproof gloves. And a pair of boots.

'Is this necessary?' demanded Kobal.

'She is in the river,' Barmella pointed out. 'She nearly dies. We do not want her to catch the cold.'

'I suppose not,' he conceded grudgingly. 'But we haven't got all day.'

He inspected Jade before they left and pulled her hood up. 'Cinderella *shall* go to the ball,' he said. 'Madam, your carriage awaits.'

She wouldn't have been surprised if it *was* a carriage but it was an SUV – a Lexus – far better than the car Aunt Em had hired. Barmella joined Jade in the back to keep a wary eye on her.

They followed the road back towards the bridge but as they swept round the final bend they saw the lights of a roadblock.

'OK. Leave this to me,' Kobal said. He caught Jade's eye in the rear-view mirror. 'And not a squeak out of you, my girl. It won't do you any good and it will only annoy me. And you know what happens when I'm annoyed. I lose all sense of fair play.'

There was a police Land Rover with flashing lights

drawn part way across the road and two policemen standing next to it. Only two. That wasn't good. They didn't even have guns. One of them came round to the driver's side and Kobal dropped the window.

'Anything wrong, officer?' he asked in his posh English voice. 'Has there been an accident?'

'We're looking for a missing child.' The officer stared at the hooded figure of Jade in the back seat but instead of making them all get out of the car he just gazed at her with a puzzled frown. Jade had seen that look before. It was as if he was trying to remember something. Like, what is a child? Or what am I doing out here at ten o'clock at night stopping cars in the pouring rain? Kobal was playing his mind games.

'As you can see my own daughter is far from well,' he said. 'We're taking her into hospital in Carlisle.'

Barmella put an arm round her while Jade looked around for the other policemen. And then she saw something that made her heart leap. Another vehicle had drawn up at the roadblock. A pick-up truck, coming from the opposite direction. The second policeman had gone over to it and he was talking to the driver. He stepped back and waved it on but then he glanced over towards the Lexus. Jade tried to picture his thoughts and put her own picture there but it was so hard to concentrate with Kobal in the front of the car and Barmella sitting right next to her. Then it dawned on her. She didn't have to play mind games. There were easier ways of drawing attention to herself.

She pressed her face against the window and pulled the most hideous idiot face she could manage. Head lolling, tongue protruding, eyes crossed and squinting. The policeman started. She made a different face, just in case he thought she couldn't help it. Then he came marching over and yanked open the car door.

'Out!' he snapped.

Kobal's head jerked round. 'What's going on?' he demanded.

'Step out of the car, please,' the policeman commanded firmly.

Jade was out of the car in a flash. She smiled at him disarmingly. The pick-up moved forward. Just as it passed them, Jade made her move.

'Hey!' The policeman grabbed at her. Barmella hurled herself forward in a rugby tackle. But they collided in mid-air and fell in a heap on the road. Jade leaped for the tailgate of the moving truck, hung on as it gathered speed, and then climbed over the top and tumbled into what smelled and felt like a heap of manure. When she looked back, the two policemen were running for their Land Rover and Kobal and Barmella were climbing back into the Lexus. The pick-up was moving quite fast now but it wouldn't be long before they caught up with her. Unless the police got there first. Then what would happen? She hoped they were calling for back-up.

The squeal of brakes and Jade was thrown into the muck again. Had the driver realized what was happening? But no, there was a larger vehicle coming towards them – a milk tanker by the look of it – and not enough room to pass in the narrow lane.

Jade seized her opportunity. She leaped down into the road, vaulted the stone wall, and ran off into the darkness. There was a terrible pain in her head, flashing lights in her eyes, a terrible weariness in her limbs and she knew it was Kobal trying to stop her but she ran on, singing out loud:

'*Good King Wenceslas looked out*
On the feast of Stephen.
When the snow lay round about,
Deep and crisp and eeeev-en . . .'

And the rain came pouring down and the wind howled around her ears and the darkness swallowed her up.

12

Lost on the Fells

Dawn. A dank, dreary dawn, creeping over the crouching fells like cold fingers, prying into every nook and cranny, probing the dark clefts and dank, dripping ravines . . . and finally finding the entrance to the old lead mine where Jade had spent the night. She was awake at once, like a startled deer, wary and alert.

But so stiff. Stiff and cold, despite her survival suit. Her whole body ached, as if she had been beaten with sticks. She climbed unsteadily to her feet and peered cautiously out on to the world. The grim, barren fells stretched before her as far as the eye could see under a mottled bruise of a sky. Not a sign of human life. She could have been on the moon. But it didn't surprise her. She had run and walked and climbed for hours before she had found the deserted mine shaft.

Now what? She took stock of her situation. Kobal would still be looking for her; but so would the police and the rescue services. It was a question of who would get to her first . . . Unless she could find her way to a house with a phone. It shouldn't be that hard, not in England. She stumbled out into the open air. It was still raining, but more of a steady drizzle than the downpour of the night before. Beyond the mine shaft, the ground climbed quite steeply to a rocky ridge. It was half hidden by cloud but she thought it might give her a better view. She forced her cramped limbs into action and began to climb, but the cloud grew thicker and before long she was stumbling through an impenetrable mist. Her boots had begun to chafe and she was desperately hungry. If the cloud had lifted and she had found herself in the grounds of Saint Severa's she would have jumped for joy. But the cloud didn't lift.

A small stream provided her with breakfast and she followed it down, slipping and sliding over the wet grass until she reached a small lake – a tarn – between hills: a lonely, barren place with only the sound of running water from every direction. She felt as if she was in a labyrinth formed not of hedges, but of mountain streams.

She began to climb again and briefly emerged from the cloud into a kind of light: a cold, grey northern light. She could see little of her surroundings but at least she could make out the sun, or rather a dim glow through the next veil of cloud. She set off a little more cheerfully and almost in response the veil lifted and she found herself looking down at a distant village – and a road.

And two figures climbing towards her.

She threw herself down in the grass but she saw one of them point in her direction so they must have seen her. But who were they? She peered through the drizzle, trying to make out their faces but they were too far away and they were wearing hoods.

It had to be them.

She climbed to her feet and began to retrace her steps up the hill as fast as she could for all the pain in her feet and the weariness in her tortured limbs. There was another torrent ahead of her but she forced herself to cross it, jumping from rock to rock as the rushing waters surged past. When she looked back she saw the two figures had split up and were coming after her, one to the right and one to the left. But then the cloud came down again and this time she was grateful for it.

It seemed darker now and she was heading away from the sun, away from the roads, back into the wilderness. Her boots were killing her but she forced herself to keep climbing. Across another stream, the cold water seeping into her boots and numbing the pain for a welcome few minutes before it started again, worse than before. Only the fear of Kobal kept her going.

And then the clouds rolled back and he was there, right ahead of her, and she swayed on her feet, too exhausted, too dispirited to run any more. And there was no point, anyway, for she was trapped between them.

Then he put up his hands and pushed back the hood and she saw his face and her knees buckled from under her and she pitched forward senseless into the wet bracken.

13

The Child of the Spirit

She was in Hell. A demon was pouring fire and brimstone down her throat. She could feel it burning its way down her chest and searing the lining of her stomach. She choked and coughed, flailing about with her hands. But the demon grabbed her by the wrist.

'Easy, easy,' he said.

She opened her eyes.

'You!'

'Who were you expecting?' he enquired with a smile.

'Where have you been?' she demanded furiously.

'I had to go to Rome,' said Benedict. 'Sorry. Have you missed me?'

Had she missed him? She hadn't realized until now just how much. She felt a sob catch in her throat – but it might have been the drink he had poured down her.

'What is that stuff?'

'Brandy.' He held up the flask. 'Sorry if it's not up to your usual standard.'

He was so like her father in some ways, and yet so different in others. He claimed to be her uncle – Kobal's brother – but she had met him only once and in such strange circumstances that if he'd said he was her guardian angel she'd have believed him. Already she felt safe and secure, even in the middle of a wilderness with the black clouds closing in and Kobal lurking in the vicinity. Then she saw he was not alone. There was another figure standing behind him, wearing a hooded anorak.

'Guess who I found on the way,' said Benedict, drawing back a little, and Jade caught a glimpse of the features under the hood.

'Aunt Em!'

Then she was on the grass beside her and their arms were around each other. Aunt Em, who never hugged or kissed.

'I thought you were dead,' they both said together

– and then they were laughing and crying at the same time.

'I thought I'd never see you again. I thought you were . . .'

'I couldn't get back to you – the river just swept me away and . . .'

'Perhaps we could save this for later,' Benedict suggested. 'When we get back to the car.'

He had left the car at the edge of the village and while Benedict drove Jade filled them in on what had happened to her since her plunge into the river. They didn't seem too surprised about her meeting with Kobal. Emily just hugged her and kissed her head. 'I thought I'd lost you,' she said. 'Oh, babe, you're so cold.'

But Jade felt warmer than she had for years.

Emily, it turned out, had been swept downriver to a small village where she had managed to crawl out and phone the police.

'We spent the night searching for you along the river,' she said. 'But I knew they thought you were dead and all they'd find was the body. Then *he* turned up – from Rome, if you please.' She shot a glance at Benedict that was almost accusing. 'He said you were still alive and you were probably lost on the fells.

I don't know what made him so sure.'

He caught Jade's eyes in the mirror. 'I had a feeling you were in trouble,' he said. 'So I got back as fast as I could.'

'How?'

The question seemed to surprise him. 'I caught the night train to Paris,' he said, 'and then flew to Edinburgh and picked up a hire car.'

Jade rolled her eyes. 'I mean how did you know I was in trouble?'

'Oh. As I say, just a gut feeling.' She might have known she'd never get a straight answer from him. 'I was on my way to the school when I ran into a police roadblock. So then I knew it was true.'

'So what now?' Jade asked.

'First the hospital,' said Emily firmly. 'Then the police.'

'Why the hospital?'

'Jade — you've been in a car crash. You've been dumped in a river. You've spent a night alone on a mountain. You want to know why the hospital?'

'But I'm fine,' Jade protested. 'Apart from my feet.'

'Even so — you need a thorough check-up. You probably need a few jabs. Maybe a brain scan wouldn't be a bad idea.'

Jade was silent for a while. Then she said: 'What shall I tell the police?'

'You could try the truth,' Emily suggested sardonically.

Jade sniffed. 'What did *you* tell them?'

'I told them your father is an escaped criminal and that he's trying to abduct you. And that we thought he was chasing us in his car.'

'That's all?'

'You don't have to go into unnecessary detail,' she said defensively.

'So no stuff about the other kids. Nothing about breeding freaks and monsters. Nothing about his incredible magic powers.'

'There's nothing magic about them,' insisted Emily. 'They're just mind games.'

'Oh, that's all right then,' said Jade sarcastically.

For the next few hours she felt like an object on an assembly line being moved from room to room, trolley to trolley, while people in white coats poked and prodded at her as if they were inspecting her for flaws. Which in a way they were. They shone lights in her eyes and in her ears and down her throat, stuck needles in her arms and her bottom, smeared ointment on her feet, tapped her knees with a small hammer and asked her loads of questions. Then they stuck her in a bed in a private room and sent the police in. There were two of them – a man and a woman.

'Well, young lady,' said the man. 'You *have* been in the wars.'

Tell me about it, thought Jade, but she just smiled at them sweetly. Emily and Benedict had come in with them, presumably to make sure the police didn't make life too difficult for her. Or, more likely, that she didn't make life too difficult for the police.

They weren't interested in the story of her amazing escape from a car in the bottom of a river, or her escape from the river itself – which was a pity because she had rehearsed that story over and over in her mind and it was getting more amazing by the minute.

Their only real interest was in Kobal. 'Your father' as they called him.

'Did he give you any idea of where he was planning to take you?' they asked.

'I think they were heading for the Lake District,' she said.

'And why would that be?'

'He probably had a seaplane on one of the lakes.'

'A seaplane?'

'Yes. You know – a plane that lands on water.'

'Yes. I, er . . . I know the type,' said the man. His smile was starting to look a little strained at the edges. 'But what makes you think your father has one?'

'Because he's got a thing about them. He always uses seaplanes if he's planning a quick getaway. Except the last time he used a Zeppelin.' She shot a glance towards Benedict but his face was expressionless.

'A Zeppelin?' said the policeman. His eyes slid towards his companion.

'You know – like a balloon, only shaped like a cigar. The Germans used them during the First World War. To bomb England.'

'Yes. So I've heard. And you say your father has one?'

'Yes. The original one – built by Count Zeppelin himself in the 1890s. But I expect he's crashed it by now. He's always crashing things,' she announced cheerfully. 'He crashed the last seaplane. On a frozen lake. I was lucky to get out alive.'

'I see.' The two police officers exchanged glances again. It was obvious they didn't believe a word of it. 'Well – I think that's . . . that's enough to be going on with. We can take a full statement later. We'll let you rest for a while. You probably need that. Yes. Plenty of rest.'

Benedict saw them out of the room.

'Brilliant,' said Aunt Em sarcastically when they'd gone. 'Just perfect. They're now convinced you're a total fruitcake. Well done.'

'I only told them the truth,' Jade insisted, 'like you told me to.'

'Well, at least it stopped them asking too many questions,' Benedict pointed out as he returned to the room.

'Oh, they'll be back, don't you worry. Or if not them, others like them – except they'll be a lot more persistent and a lot less friendly.'

'Why?' Jade felt aggrieved. 'What have I done wrong?'

'Jade, it's not a question of what you've done wrong.' Emily sighed. 'Look, your father's activities have attracted a lot of attention in high places. Some people have become very alarmed – not only about him but . . .' she hesitated '. . . about certain of his "experiments".'

'Experiments? You mean me. Me and the other kids. The freak show.'

'Jade. You are not a freak. Listen . . . Look at me and don't go all sulky. You have to look at it from their point of view. Your father appears to be able to read people's minds. Not only that but, well, to *control* their minds, to some extent. He can put the fear of death into them, or – or he can make them believe what he *wants* them to believe, see things he *wants* them to see . . . I don't know how it works but . . . whatever it is, he seems to have passed it on to you. You and the rest of his children. Can't you see how scary that is? Think of the crimes you could commit, the people you could influence. It's a matter of national security.'

'We can't all do it,' explained Jade sullenly. 'And it gives you a terrible headache.'

'Oh, that's a relief. I'll tell them that. I expect they'll stop bothering you and go back to worrying about less important things – like terrorism and stopping the spread of nuclear weapons.'

'Who are "*they*"?' Benedict enquired mildly.

'Certain colleagues of mine in government,' replied Emily in a tone that said mind your own business.

'And they're interested in Jade?'

'Yes. I'm afraid they are. One of the reasons I let

her go to this school of yours was because it kept her out of the limelight. Unfortunately this has put her right back in it again. It's only a matter of time before they get on their bikes and come tearing up here. If they're not on their way already.'

'And what will they do when they get here?'

'Well, they'll want to question her of course and . . . I don't know . . . but they may want to place her in a more . . . a more secure environment.'

'You mean lock me up,' said Jade, who had been listening to this exchange with growing alarm. 'Shut me up in prison. Or mental hospital. Like they did to *him*. Keep me on drugs or do things to my brain so I won't be a problem for them.'

Emily turned to her. 'Is that what Kobal told you they'd do?'

Jade didn't answer.

'Jade – people don't want to hurt you but . . . you scare people. And when people are scared sometimes they . . . sometimes they overreact.'

'By looking them up in a secure environment,' said Benedict, 'and screwing around with their brains.'

Emily whirled round on him, eyes blazing. 'You can talk,' she said. 'What would you do? Lock her in a convent guarded by a crowd of crazy old nuns?

Sprinkle her with holy water and hang a bunch of garlic round her neck and a crucifix?'

'That's not quite what I had in mind,' Benedict pointed out, 'but personally I'd prefer it to brain surgery.'

'I don't *try* to scare people,' said Jade in a small voice. A brief image of Jasmine sprang to mind with her hand in a bucket of water and Rose lying in the corridor next to her, but she hastily wiped it from her vision. 'I didn't want this to happen. I didn't want to be different . . .' Actually this wasn't true. She had always wanted to be different. Until she found out she *was*. 'I just want to be left alone.'

Emily put her arm around her. 'I know, sweetheart,' she said. 'I know.' She glared at Benedict.

'OK, OK,' he said. 'Let's not fall out among ourselves. Kobal is the real problem here. We need to know what he wants with these kids. Then maybe we can do something about it.'

'He says he wants us to save the world,' said Jade.

'Well – lucky old world,' said Emily.

'I wouldn't have said that was a pressing concern of his,' said Benedict. 'Not as long as *I've* known him.'

'So what *does* he want with us, then?'

'That's what we have to find out. But let's

just think about what we *do* know. There are seven of you. And for some reason he wants you all together. Why?'

'Well, I think we can rule out the idea of being a big happy family,' said Emily. 'Sorry, Jade, but he's not what I'd call a natural parent.'

'We haven't seen much evidence of it in the past,' Benedict agreed. 'No, I think it might have something to do with what he thinks the seven of you can achieve, with his guidance. Multiplying your considerable talents.'

'Our talents?' Jade regarded him warily.

'Your powers or your energies, or whatever you like to call them.'

'In what way?'

'OK. There are seven children from seven different places – right? What are seven sevens?'

It didn't take much talent to work that out. 'Forty-nine?' Jade suggested.

'Not in Kobal's book. According to Kobal, seven sevens makes six hundred and sixty-six.' He took a notebook out of his pocket and wrote down a sum.

$$777 - \frac{777}{7} = 666$$

131

'Great,' said Jade, with a shrug. 'But what does it mean?'

'Well, according to the Bible, or rather, certain scholars who make a study of the Bible, six–six–six is the number of the Beast. Otherwise known as Abaddon: the Angel of the Abyss who will rise to rule the world in its final days.'

Emily made a dismissive noise but Jade stared at him in amazement. 'He said something about that. In the house. Yesterday.' Was it only yesterday? It seemed an age ago. She frowned, trying to remember. 'Something about seven angels with seven trumpets . . . and a star that would fall to earth and . . .' She tried to recall his exact words . . .

' "*And they shall have as king over them the Angel of the Abyss whose name is Abaddon*",' quoted Benedict.

'Mad,' said Emily, shaking her head.

'Maybe,' he conceded. 'But there's usually a certain logic to his reasoning. Maybe he thinks that the seven of you, united, will give him some kind of power – like the Angel of the Abyss – the power to rule the world.'

'Look, he's mad, bad and dangerous to know,' Emily agreed, 'but he's not that dangerous. He's not going to rule the world, even with Jade and the rest of the family to help him.'

'Maybe not. But he could do a lot of damage on the way. A lot of damage to the kids in particular.'

Emily brooded on this for a moment.

'So how do we stop him?'

'Well, one way would be to find the missing child before he does.'

'How?'

'OK – we know they all have some connection with the Septagram – Kobal's favourite sign, the seven-pointed star. That each of the points has a name and each child is linked with it by birth or some other kind of association.' He had the names written down in his notebook: the seven points of the star. 'Forest, Fire, Sea, Wind, Moon, Magic – and Spirit. Jade was born in a forest, Paco at the foot of a volcano and so on. So where does the seventh child come from? The Child of the Spirit. Where is the place of the Spirit?'

'It could be anywhere in the world,' Emily pointed out.

'Romania,' said Jade.

Benedict looked sharply at her. 'What makes you think that?'

'Because he told me. He said the kid was

Romanian. A Romanian gypsy boy.'

'He *told* you?' He frowned. 'Why would he have done that? Told you the one thing he wouldn't want us to know?'

'He didn't know she'd escape,' put in Emily. 'And that we'd find her.'

'True,' he mused. But he didn't seem convinced. 'He wanted you to help him, didn't he?' he said to Jade. 'To help find this Romanian gypsy boy. Like you helped him find the others.'

Jade flushed. Helping Kobal find the others was not something she was proud of.

'But why would he need Jade?' Emily protested.

'I don't know. Maybe because he wanted to make her a part of what he's trying to do. Maybe because she can do some things he can't.'

'Like what?'

'Use her imagination.'

'What?'

'Imagination. Surely you've heard of it. Or isn't it something recognized by modern science? I'm sorry. Put it this way. Jade has got something he hasn't. A powerful imagination. Maybe he had it once but he lost it. Like most adults, to some extent.'

'He said it was my subconscious leading me

to them,' Jade remembered. 'But I don't know how it works.'

'Do you know what I mean by parallel worlds?' Benedict asked her.

'Other worlds that are, like, running alongside our own but you can't see them? Only sometimes you can sense them.'

'Well, that's a bit like the way your subconscious works. Other worlds running side by side, in your head. And sometimes you can reach through to them. Under hypnosis for instance. Or they reach through to you. Like in books, where people step into a parallel world almost by accident, through a magic keyhole, or a wardrobe, or a hole in space. Some people are better at it than others. You seem to be one of them. Kobal can feed you with information. He can show you images – on a computer, for instance. He can make you an avatar in a computer game – and your imagination does the rest. Except in your case it's rather more than that. You can see where they are, you can feel what they're feeling – it's like you're there with them. Isn't that right?'

She nodded, but she was chewing on her lip as she remembered how her father had made her help him find the others.

'There's nothing to be ashamed of,' he assured her, shaking his head. 'It's just a talent you have, a kind of ESP.'

'E-what?'

'Extra-sensory perception. Something even scientists recognize . . .' A glance at Emily. 'They think that in the past, in the distant past, when we lived in caves, many people had it but over the years it was lost to us, or faded, like a tail. Now only a very few people have it. You have a particularly powerful version of it . . .' He paused. Then he added gently: 'That's how Kobal found the others, isn't it?'

'Some of them,' she admitted cautiously, 'but only because he made me.'

'But not the seventh.'

'No. He blocked me out.'

'Who blocked you out?'

'Number seven. It was like, he didn't want me to find him.'

'But before that, before he blocked you out – what did you see?'

She tried to remember. 'Mountains. Snow. A path. Into the clouds.'

'What else?'

She shook her head. 'Nothing.'

'Are you sure?'

Then she remembered. 'There was a castle.'

'A castle?'

'I think it was a castle. I only saw it for a second, then the clouds rolled back.'

'A castle – or a monastery?'

She shook her head, confused.

'But if you saw it again . . . would you recognize it?'

'Why are you doing this,' Emily demanded. Then she caught his eye. 'No,' she said firmly. 'No. Definitely not. Not in a million years.'

14

Escape

The best time to escape from a hospital, according to Benedict, was just after the night shift came on duty.

'We'll all go to jail,' Emily moaned.

'Trust me,' said Benedict.

This did nothing to reassure her.

A few minutes after seven a new nurse came round to check Jade's temperature. She looked at them enquiringly.

'We're just going,' said Benedict. Emily kissed Jade goodnight and said she'd see her in the morning. Then they left. Five minutes after the nurse had gone they were back – wearing white coats and pushing a wheelchair.

'Get in,' Benedict told Jade urgently, 'and

put that over your head.'

He threw her what looked like a plastic shower cap.

She viewed it with disgust. 'I'm not wearing that,' she said.

He frowned at her fiercely. 'Just put it on and get in the wheelchair.' He grabbed the shower cap and pulled it down over her ears. 'If anyone stops us just drool like an idiot. You should find that easy. Leave the talking to me.'

She scowled. Sometimes he sounded just like Kobal.

He wheeled her out into the corridor with Emily running ahead to open doors. They didn't see any police or security guards and no one tried to stop them. Benedict wheeled her right out into the car park and lifted her into the back of the car.

'Your clothes are on the seat,' he said. 'Put them on over your pyjamas. And if they stop us at the gate don't make faces at anyone.'

She stared at him in astonishment. 'How did you know . . . ?'

'ESP,' he said with a wink.

Emily was scandalized there were no police.

'They could have just walked in there and

grabbed her at any time,' she said. 'I've a good mind to make a complaint.'

'I'll drive you to the police station, shall I?' said Benedict. 'You won't mind if we wait outside.'

He drove them to the railway station. It looked deserted.

'Where are we going?' Emily wanted to know.

'London. On the Caledonian Sleeper. I like sleepers,' he informed Jade confidentially. 'I like trains generally. In my view it's the only civilized way to travel . . .' He considered for a moment. 'At least since they took the *Queen Mary* off the New York run.'

'Excuse me?' Emily was looking at him as if he was losing it.

'Ocean liner,' he explained. 'Built in 1929 for the Atlantic crossing. Now a floating hotel in Long Beach.'

'Yes,' she said faintly. 'I think I probably knew that. And the sleeper?'

'Train that you sleep in. It arrives in ten minutes.'

'Oh, yes.' Emily looked pointedly at the deserted station. 'And you think it's going to stop here, do you?' She laughed dryly. 'There won't be another train in this station until tomorrow morning,' she said. 'Trust me.'

Ten minutes later the Caledonian Sleeper glided to a stop in front of her. Emily stared at it as if it was the *Queen Mary*. Benedict shot off to find the train manager.

'It's almost empty,' he told them when he came back. 'I've got us two adjoining sleepers in first class.'

It was the first time Jade had been on a sleeper. She was not sure it was the *only* civilized way to travel but it was a lot better than spending the night on a bench on Carlisle station or a deserted mine shaft on the fells. She even managed to get some sleep. They arrived in London just after five in the morning and slept on till just after seven, when the attendant awoke them with tea and biscuits – and a note from Benedict.

Things to do, it said. *Meet me under the clock at St Pancras at 0900 hours.*

The station clock at St Pancras was probably the most famous meeting place in London. It was so famous they'd erected a giant statue to mark the site. Called, predictably, the Meeting Place. It was of a couple kissing. Jade felt embarrassed standing next to it; it was so wet. She wondered if the other fifty or sixty people standing there felt the same way.

141

'He might have chosen somewhere a bit less public,' muttered Emily under her breath. 'And where is he, anyway?'

It was already ten past nine.

'I don't know why I'm doing this,' she said for about the hundredth time. 'I must be as mad as he is.'

Jade peered over the rail into the station precinct below. It was packed with people rushing to work. She suddenly thought of her foster father, who always left for work about this time. Rush hour, every day of his life. She found herself looking for him in the crowd: a tubby little man with ginger hair and a moustache, who walked with a brisk, busy stride. But he had no reason to be anywhere near St Pancras because he worked as a civil servant at the Home Office and caught the District Line every morning from Turnham Green to St James's Park. Once, when she was a little girl, he had told her he was a burglar and for a while she had believed him. She smiled at this, now, because it seemed like it was the only time they had been at all close. The rest of the time she was growing up he had seemed a remote, rather self-important figure who hardly ever spoke to her, or even noticed that she was there. He was better than her mother, though – or rather, her foster mother. Jade hadn't hit it off with her at all. They were so unalike – physically and in every other way – it seemed amazing now that she had ever believed either of them were her real parents. But she had. Or, at least, she had never entertained any serious doubts on the subject. Up to a few months ago. Until then she had been entirely convinced that she was the only daughter of a tubby, ginger-haired civil servant who hardly ever spoke to her and a pale, thin woman who worked part-time as a dental receptionist and never stopped nagging. She hadn't really wanted to be that person. She hadn't really wanted those parents. She hadn't really been at all happy, now she came to think about it. In fact she had been quite unhappy a lot of the time. But she had felt safe. Secure. Normal. Even boringly normal.

And now? Now she didn't know who she was. Or what.

'He's probably been arrested,' hissed Aunt Em in her ear.

'Who?'

'Benedict. Who do you think?'

'Why should he be arrested?' Jade hissed back at her.

'Oh, abduction of a minor will do for starters, don't you think?'

'He hasn't abducted me – yet.'

'Oh, no? I don't recall any of the medics signing you out of hospital, do you? Or did it happen when I had to run to the loo before I wet myself. Ah – at last!'

Benedict was hurrying towards them with a backpack and two suitcases.

'What kept you?' Emily demanded.

'I'll explain later,' he said. He put the suitcases down and pulled a fat bundle out of his pocket. 'Here're your tickets.'

Emily glanced down at them. They were for the 10.23 Eurostar to Paris.

'Why are we going to Paris?' Emily asked, keeping her voice low.

'Because Paris is where we catch the fast train to Munich. And Munich is where we catch the night train to Budapest. And Budapest is where we catch the slow train to Romania. OK?'

'And then what?'

'Then we find the monastery.'

'What monastery?' asked Jade.

'Look, we don't have time for this. I'll

explain on the train.'

'We're going all the way to Romania *by train*?' Emily looked at him in astonishment.

'We are. Isn't that exciting?'

'But – why can't we fly?'

'A – because trains are better for the environment; B – because the security isn't as tight in stations as it is at airports; and C – because I don't like flying. It's not natural. Here.' He handed them a suitcase each. 'I suggest you change in the Ladies'. You've got ten minutes.'

'Change?' Emily looked stunned. 'Change into what?'

'The clothes in the suitcase.'

'What's wrong with the clothes we're wearing?'

'You might be recognized.' He dived into his pocket again. 'Oh, and here are your new passports.'

Jade's was in the name of someone called Margaret Jane Johnson. It showed a young girl with long black pigtails and glasses and a goofy grin.

'It looks nothing like me,' she protested.

'It will,' Benedict assured her, 'when you put on your disguise. It's in the suitcase.'

'No!' There was a small explosion from Emily. She was staring at her own passport photo in horror.

'Never! You have got to be kidding me.'

'Ten minutes,' said Benedict firmly. 'Unless you want us to leave without you.'

Fifteen minutes later two figures emerged from the Ladies' at St Pancras Station. One was a young girl with glasses and pigtails and a goofy grin. The other was a nun.

'Don't,' warned Emily when she caught Benedict's eye. 'Not a single word. And *you* can stop grinning like an idiot,' she told Jade. 'You look like Bugs Bunny in drag.'

'I'm not grinning,' said Jade. 'It's my teeth.'

She had two plastic front teeth over her real ones. Even with her mouth closed they protruded slightly over her bottom lip. It was difficult to talk properly. She thought eating might be a problem too.

'All I was going to say is that if anyone asks, you're one of the Poor Sisters of Clare,' Benedict told Emily. 'And remember, if you make the sign of the cross it's left shoulder before right.' He demonstrated for her.

'Why would I want to make the sign of the cross?' Emily asked him,

'Oh, I don't know, it's a nun thing. Come on.' He shouldered his backpack. 'And if they do stop us—'

'We know,' they said together, 'leave the talking to you.'

But as they moved off from under the statue neither of them noticed the two men in the crowd who, after exchanging a brief but significant glance, followed them at a discreet distance as they headed towards passport control.

15

The Man in the Black Hat

They glided through the Kent countryside at 186 miles an hour. Jade knew the exact speed because Benedict told her. He seemed to have a thing about trains.

'You can have no idea what it was like before they were invented,' he said.

It was the first time Jade had travelled by Eurostar. In fact it would be the first time she'd ever been out of the country, apart from the time she'd been kidnapped by her father. All her holidays had been spent in England and Wales. She had thought little of this at the time – if anyone had asked she would have said her parents didn't like going abroad – but now she wondered if there had been a more sinister reason and that she hadn't been allowed to leave the country. She had never even held a passport – the one she had now, in the name of Margaret Johnson was the first she'd ever seen. But it hadn't caused any problems at passport control.

Emily thought it was all a bit too easy.

'Why shouldn't it be easy?' Benedict shrugged. 'Thousands of people pass through St Pancras every day.'

'But they'll know she's gone missing from the hospital.' Emily dropped her voice, even though they had a table to themselves and the carriage was half empty. 'There'll be looking for her everywhere – especially every exit point.'

'They'll be looking for a child called Jade Connor, or at least a child answering her description,' Benedict pointed out. 'Not a girl called Margaret Johnson looking like . . .' he glanced across at Jade '. . . Bugs Bunny.'

Jade smiled obligingly, showing her front teeth. Emily winced.

'Well, I don't know. I think they've been told to let her through,' she muttered darkly. 'So she'll lead them to the others.'

'Who's they?' asked Jade curiously.

'The police. Or MI5.'

'Why don't you give them a ring and ask them?' suggested Benedict dryly.

Emily wasn't amused. 'Just because I work for the government doesn't mean I'm a spook,' she hissed.

She lapsed into a huffy silence, staring out of the window, but even though Jade knew Benedict hadn't been entirely serious it had started her thinking. Aunt Em mightn't be a *spook*, precisely – she didn't work for the secret police, at least so far as Jade knew – but she *was* employed by the government and her work *was* secret. And it had something to do with Jade. So what was she doing dressed up as a nun, traipsing across Europe? Keeping an eye on her? Reporting back to whoever she worked for?

There was one sure way of finding out.

She could read her mind.

Jade felt the blood drain from her face. It would be such an awful thing to do. Like prying. Worse, like stealing from a friend, or one of your own family.

But if it was in self-defence?

No. She shook her head fiercely. This was Kobal, trying to trick her into doing something she knew was wrong. Of it if wasn't Kobal, exactly, it was the part of Kobal that was also part of her. The evil part.

Besides, reading people's minds wasn't that easy. People's minds were complicated, even more complicated than computers. They were capable of thinking many different thoughts at once. Mind-reading was like peering into a rock pool with vague thoughts darting about like fish in the murky depths. And sometimes you caught the wrong one. As Kobal had once told her, you could read the mind of a serial killer while he was thinking about his dinner and all you'd get was a meat pie. Unless he was thinking of eating his next victim.

He'd told her he'd teach her to be better at it but he never had. Maybe she should be grateful for that.

Putting thoughts into people's minds was a different matter, though. That wasn't like prying, or stealing. That was . . . fun. But it was also wrong. She knew that. Unless your life depended on it. Or people like Rose and Jasmine were making it extremely difficult for you. And even then, it wasn't right.

There was no way she was going to use her dubious talents on Aunt Em. She just had to hope she could trust her.

The train was slowing down. The train manager made an announcement in English and French to tell

151

them they were about to enter the Channel Tunnel.

Benedict looked at his watch. 'Anyone for drinks?' he asked. 'Or something to eat?'

'Just a second,' said Emily firmly. 'Now we've got a moment, perhaps you'll kindly tell us why we're going to Romania.'

He looked at her in surprise. 'You know why we're going to Romania. To find the Child of the Spirit.'

'Just like that. And how long do you think it's going to take? I mean, just so I know how long I have to dress up as a nun.'

'Well, that depends on what we find when we get there.'

She shook her head. 'Not good enough,' she said. 'If you don't tell us more than that we're getting off at Paris.'

'OK.' He lowered his voice. 'We're looking for a monastery.'

'I gathered that,' said Emily acidly, 'but—'

'A particular monastery. The Monastery of the Holy Spirit. Or the Holy Ghost. A community of Orthodox monks. They've been around for centuries but in recent years they were established in a town called Bistrita, in Transylvania. They used to run an orphanage there.'

'And you think this is the monastery Jade saw, in her imagination or whatever?' Benedict nodded. 'And this kid, this Child of the Spirit, was one of the orphans?'

'I do. But a few years ago the orphanage was closed down and the monks disappeared.'

'Disappeared?'

'They went somewhere else. No one knows where exactly – that's one of the things I was checking in London – but it's thought they're still somewhere in the same area.'

'And you think Jade will know it when she sees it?'

'I'm hoping she'll recognize some of the landmarks. Or . . . or find it by some other means.' He stood up. 'Now what can I get you?'

'I suppose a gin and tonic's out of the question,' said Emily sardonically.

'Well, it's not a nun's regular tipple, as far as I know. Not at eleven in the morning. And I think the Poor Sisters of Clare are more into Baileys. But I could put it into a plastic cup and pretend it's water.'

'A coffee will do,' Emily replied shortly. 'Jade?'

'Can I take my teeth out?'

'No,' said Benedict. 'Not until we reach Paris.'

They were out of the Channel Tunnel before Benedict came back with the drinks.

'What kept you?' Emily demanded.

'I thought I'd have a bit of a wander,' he said. He seemed distracted. 'And I saw a man in a hat.'

'I see.' Emily didn't seem overly impressed. 'Bully for you. What kind of a hat?'

'A black hat,' said Benedict. 'The kind known as a fedora. Made in Italy. With a wide brim, bent over at the front.'

'Well, I suppose it is a bit unusual these days, particularly on a train,' Emily conceded. 'But compared to a Vogon from the Planet Vogsphere, say, or the Poisonous Serpent of Septicaemia, I wouldn't say it was especially alarming, would you?'

'If he's the man I think he is, it's very alarming. And a lot more poisonous than – what was it . . . ?'

'Why?' Emily frowned. 'Who is he?'

'If I'm right, his name is Mancini. *One* of his names, anyway. Most people call him Bardolino, after the people who make the hats. It's his trademark – among certain members of the criminal community.'

'He's a criminal? What kind of criminal?' Jade was more curious than alarmed.

'He kills people,' Benedict informed her mildly.

'He's a hit man for one of the leading Mafia families in Sicily.'

'Oh, well, that's a relief,' said Emily. 'I thought he might be a shoplifter.'

But her eyes slid warningly to Jade, whose eyes were as wide as saucers.

'Mafia?' she repeated wonderingly. 'You mean *the* Mafia?'

'It's a kind of generic term,' Benedict replied matter-of-factly. 'It describes a multitude of sins – and sinners. And in this case I suspect he's working on a private contract.'

'A contract? You mean, like a contract to kill people?'

'That kind of thing,' Benedict agreed carelessly. 'But as I say, I don't think killing is involved. Not for the moment.'

'Great,' said Emily faintly. 'You'll tell us, will you, if the situation changes?'

'You can count on it,' he grinned.

'So who's he working for? Kobal?'

'No. For once I don't think Kobal is involved. I rather suspect it's one of my colleagues in the Church.'

'Right,' said Emily. 'The Church. Sh⟨o⟩ have known.'

'It's not something they'd want you or anyone else to know,' he assured her. 'But I'm afraid certain members of the Order have had links with the Mafia in the past. They're probably hoping we'll lead them to the other kids.'

'And then what?'

'*Then* they'll kill us.'

He winked at Jade as if it was a huge joke.

'So who *are* these colleagues of yours?' Emily demanded sharply.

'I can't be certain, but I think one of them is a man called Brother Alois. A German member of the Order. Very old and set in his ways. He thinks Kobal's the Devil.'

'And the Mafia are perfect saints I suppose?'

'Brother Alois would see them as a necessary evil,' Benedict replied.

'So what are we going to do about this Bandy Leo?' asked Jade.

'Bardolino,' Benedict corrected her mildly. 'He wouldn't like being called Bandy Leo. In fact he'd be quite cross.'

'Still, it's a good question,' Emily agreed. 'What *are* you going to do about it? Or are you perfectly happy with this arrangement?'

'No, I'm not happy at all,' Benedict said, though in fact he was smiling. 'In fact when we reach Paris I'm going to do something about it.'

'Like what?' They both asked together. Jade had seen Benedict fight once before and she was rather looking forward to seeing it again.

'I'll tell you when we get there,' he said. 'But I take it neither of you is particularly scared of the dark?'

They looked at each other.

'What kind of dark?' asked Jade warily.

'The darkness of the tomb,' said Benedict – and this time he wasn't smiling.

16

The Empire of the Dead

'I always imagined taking you to Paris when you were old enough,' Emily reflected moodily as the Eurostar slid into the Gare du Nord. 'We were going to stay at a lovely little hotel I know on the Île Saint Louis and do all the sights. Notre Dame, the Eiffel Tower, a boat trip along the Seine, lunch in Montmartre . . .'

'*Were* you? Honestly?' Jade queried her with a catch in her throat. When she was very little Aunt Em used to take her on trips into London. She had taken her to Madame Tussaud's and the zoo in Regent's Park and to see the Christmas grotto at Selfridges. But then for some reason she'd stopped and grown more distant, as if there was a barrier between them.

'Well, here you are,' Benedict announced cheerfully as the train came gently to a halt. 'Paris. And nearly four hours to kill.'

'If someone doesn't kill us first,' muttered Emily darkly.

'Don't worry, I don't think that's going to be too much of a problem on this trip,' he assured her, as if it was a small local inconvenience, like mosquitoes or sand flies, 'but I'm afraid we won't have much time for the sights.'

He left them on the station concourse while he dumped their bags in left-luggage. Jade looked around for the man in the hat but she couldn't see him, not in the kind of hat Benedict had described. She wondered if he really existed. She thought she could trust Benedict, but she couldn't be sure. She didn't really know if she could trust anyone.

When he returned she noticed he'd kept his own bag, his backpack. And he'd bought three tickets for the Paris Metro.

'Where are we going?' Emily wanted to know.

'Porte de l'Enfer,' he told her. 'Stay close and don't keep looking over your shoulder,' he instructed Jade, who was doing exactly that.

'What does Porte de l'Enfer mean?' she asked

as they followed him down the stairs to the Underground.

'The Gate of the Inferno,' Emily said, raising her eyes to the ceiling. 'Or I suppose you could say, the Gateway to Hell.'

'Did you see the man in the hat?' Jade hissed to Benedict as they stood waiting for the train.

'I did. And he met two other men. They're standing halfway along the platform. Don't look,' he added warningly.

Jade sighed. 'Can I take my teeth out now?' she asked after a moment.

'I suppose so. If you must. But don't let anyone see you.'

Jade slid them out under her palm and put them in her pocket just as the train came shaking and rattling out of the tunnel.

'So what's the deal at the Gateway to Hell?' she asked Benedict brightly.

'The deal is you stick very close to me and you don't touch the skulls,' he told her.

'Right. Stick close to you and don't touch the skulls,' Jade repeated. She flicked a meaningful glance at Aunt Em, but she was practising the sign of the cross.

160

★ ★ ★

Porte de l'Enfer turned out to be a roundabout on the Paris ring road – the Peripherique.

'It used to be one of gates in the old city wall,' Benedict told them as they watched the traffic thundering past. 'Where people had to pay taxes on everything they took in and out of the city.'

'So why have you brought us here?' enquired Emily coldly.

'Because it's also the entrance to a labyrinth,' Benedict explained mysteriously, 'and labyrinths are very handy places for losing people in.'

He led them down another subway and up into a much quieter side street with shops and restaurants. There was nothing remotely resembling the Gateway to Hell, or even a labyrinth.

'There,' said Benedict, nodding across the road.

Jade saw what appeared to be a small black hut on the corner. In its very insignificance she sensed something truly weird and creepy. But inside there was nothing more sinister than a glass-fronted ticket counter with a woman sitting inside it, reading a book. Benedict gave her some money and she gave them three tickets and pointed to a spiral staircase, leading down.

'I thought there was no such thing as Hell,' Jade muttered as they began their descent. It didn't come out quite as strongly as she intended. She had to clear her throat.

'Well, the Christian Churches seem to have revised their opinion of late,' Benedict agreed. 'At least some of the more liberal ones. If Hell does exist, the current belief is that it's more of a state of mind than an actual physical place, certainly not a place of eternal torment as we used to believe. No fire and brimstone or demons with red-hot pitchforks. But let's face it, how can you know unless you've been there?'

'So is that the purpose of our little expedition?' enquired Emily. She seemed her usual sardonic self but Jade could tell she was nervous.

'Oh, this isn't Hell,' Benedict laughed. 'It's more a kind of waiting room. A place they park the bodies, until the Resurrection. A kind of . . . left-luggage.'

They reached the bottom of the stairs and he led them down a long, dimly lit tunnel at the end of which was an archway with a sign above that read: *Arrête! C'est ici l'Empire de la Mort.*

'This,' Benedict translated, 'is the Empire of the Dead.'

The tunnel continued beyond the archway but there were fewer lights and for a moment Jade's eyes struggled to adjust to the darkness. But then she saw them . . . Human skulls. Hundreds, maybe thousands of them. They stretched along both sides of the tunnel to a height of about two metres for as far as the eye could see: line upon line of grinning skulls and empty eye sockets, glaring balefully upon the intruder, as if to deter any living creature that dared disturb their slumber, the eternal sleep of the dead.

'My God,' breathed Emily. 'What *is* this place?'

'The catacombs. They were originally dug for the limestone – like coal mines. Most of the old city was built of limestone, still is as far as I know. This is where they got it from. But it was all used up by the end of the eighteenth century and they decided to put the tunnels to a different use.'

He walked on and they followed, wondering. Down the long tunnel and into a great cavern, like an auditorium, entirely lined with skulls and bones, rising up above them like people in a theatre: an audience of the dead. Jade turned round and round and the grinning faces swam before her until she grew dizzy. Instead of applause there was the drip drip of water.

'There must be millions of them,' she said.

'Six million,' Benedict informed her. 'Give or take a few thousand.'

'But that's more than the entire population of Paris,' Emily protested.

'I know. The dead far outnumber the living. And not only in Paris.' Benedict gazed about him and Jade thought she knew what he was thinking – *So this is what it is like to be dead*. Perhaps, all things considered, he might prefer living. 'They go back several centuries – some even further.'

'But how did they get here?'

'They were moved here. At the end of the eighteenth century. The old medieval graveyards were filled to overflowing. There were bodies poking up out of the ground, falling into the sewers, even people's cellars. So they decided to rebury them. They moved them out at night, by the cartload, led by priests and monks with torches, chanting psalms. Then came the French Revolution and they brought them here straight from the guillotine. They reckon the King of France is here somewhere and Queen Marie Antoinette and most of the people who killed them. All jumbled together so you can't tell the difference. King or commoner, they're all the same in the Empire of the Dead.'

Jade selected one particular skull and peered into the empty eye sockets, trying to imagine who it had been when it was alive. Male or female? Rich or poor? Happy or sad? . . . Had life been worth living, had leaving it been painful or was the grave a welcome release? And where was it now, the creature that had once inhabited this empty shell? Or was this it, was this all there was? . . . But for once she couldn't read its thoughts.

'What you see here is just for show,' Benedict went on. 'There are places where they're just heaped up in great piles, like heaps of rubbish. Whole caverns full of them. You have to crawl over them in the dark.' Jade stared at him in astonishment. 'You get used to it,' he said. 'Like crawling over stones.'

'You've seen them? You've been there.'

He didn't answer directly. 'The catacombs are used for other purposes, not quite as innocent as tourism. They were used for smuggling in the past and as hideouts for outlaws. The French Resistance used them in the Second World War and now . . . now they're used by the catophiles.'

'The *catophiles*?' It sounded like some kind of animal. Jade looked nervously up towards the roof.

'The people who explore them. Like cavers or potholers.' He shrugged. 'It's illegal of course, but it happens.'

They had almost forgotten their own purpose in coming here. But now they heard something, something other than the dripping water from the roof. Footsteps. Coming down the tunnel towards them.

'Quick,' said Benedict. 'Through here.'

He led them down the next tunnel and into another cavern. But this one had two archways leading off it. One open, the other barred by a metal gate stretching from roof to floor.

It was this one that appeared to interest Benedict, although it was locked with a massive padlock and didn't look as if it had been opened in years. Jade peered though the bars – into another tunnel. But not lit like the others.

'Where does it go?' she asked Benedict.

But he wasn't listening. He seemed to be counting the skulls nearest to him. Then he reached inside one of the empty eye sockets and pulled out a key.

'You've been here before?'

'Once or twice,' he admitted. He fitted the key into the lock and turned. The gate opened with a ghostly creak.

Jade peered down the dark corridor. She thought she could make out eyes glinting in the darkness and hear the squealing of rats.

'You want us to go in there?'

'No, *I'm* going in there. *You're* going straight on. Quick. Before they get here.'

Jade could hear the footsteps approaching.

'Do you want us to close the gate after you?'

'No, I don't. Leave it exactly as it is. Now go.'

Emily grabbed her by the arm and they hurried across the floor of the cavern and down the passage at the far side. But after a few steps Jade wriggled free and ran back to the corner.

'Jade!' Emily hissed in alarm. 'What are you doing?'

Jade flattened herself against the wall and peered into the cavern. There was no sign of Benedict. But the footsteps were louder and suddenly they were there. Three of them, led by the man in the hat, the man Benedict had called Bardolino. He hurried over to the open gate and they began to talk rapidly, waving their arms about. Then Bardolino and one of the others entered the tunnel, leaving the third man outside, as if on guard. For what seemed an age, there was nothing. Then they heard a shout. A single shout. Then silence.

'Eh, Capo!' called the man they'd left behind. He pulled something from inside his jacket and took a step down the tunnel.

'He's got a gun,' Jade hissed.

Emily tried to pull her away but Jade wrenched free and stepped into the open.

'Hey!' she shouted.

The man whirled round, raising the gun. Then Benedict stepped out of the shadows and slugged him in the side of the head. He went down like a sack of coal.

'Yes!' Jade punched the air and did a little victory dance.

'Jade!' Emily punched her in the shoulder. 'Are you mad? You could have been killed.'

'I was only trying to distract him,' Jade explained, rubbing her shoulder and glaring indignantly.

'Thank you,' said Benedict. 'But next time, please do as you're told.' He picked the man up and slung him through the gate.

'What happened to the other two?' Jade asked, peering down the tunnel.

'I knocked them on the head,' Benedict replied simply. He slammed the gate shut and turned the key in the lock. 'They can keep the sewer rats company.

They've a lot in common.'

He half turned away and then there was a sudden blinding flash from out of the darkness and an ear-splitting bang that echoed around the chamber like a thunderclap. Benedict staggered back with a look of surprise on his face. Then he fell.

Jade screamed as she saw the hole in his jacket and the spreading stain. She ran over to him where he lay on the floor and began to pull at him, trying to drag him out of the line of fire.

Another flash and one of the skulls shattered in the row behind them.

'Get her out of here!' Benedict's voice was weak but he fixed Emily with a commanding glare. 'Get her out of here – now!'

17

Night Train to Budapest

Jade was bundled along the tunnel, too stunned to protest. The gunshots echoed inside her head. She couldn't think straight. It had all seemed such an adventure, not to be taken too seriously. But now Benedict was lying there in the darkness with a bullet in his chest.

'We've got to go back for him,' she insisted.

'Jade!'

But Jade was gone. She ran back down the tunnel towards the cavern, round the corner . . . and straight into a tall figure that loomed out of the darkness. She yelled and began to beat at it with her fists. But her wrists were held in a powerful grip.

'Why don't you ever do as you're told?'

'Benedict!'

'Who did you think it was – the Phantom of the Opera?'

He was a phantom all right. But he felt solid enough. She stepped back and stared at him in disbelief. She could see the hole in his jacket and a great red stain on his shirt. But it didn't seem to be bothering him.

'How . . . ?' she began. 'What . . . ?'

'Let's get out of here,' he said. 'We've got a train to catch.'

The train was waiting for them at the Gare d'Est. 'The fastest train in the world,' Benedict announced as if he was the proud owner. The TGV-Est from Paris to Munich. 'Broke the world speed record in July 2007,' he said. 'Reached three-hundred-and-fifty-seven miles an hour.' He gazed from the window as they flashed through the vineyards of Champagne, stark and almost barren now after the October wine harvest. 'I expect we're doing a bit less now – probably only about two hundred – but we'll be in Munich in just over six hours.' He shook his head. 'Paris to Munich in six hours. Ridiculous. Do you know how long it used to take? Almost a week post chaise – if you didn't get stuck in the snow. Even by train it took a day and a night.'

Jade and Emily exchanged glances. His eyes shone with wonderment. It seemed more incredible to him than surviving a bullet in the chest. They could still see the hole in his leather jacket where it had gone in but there was no sign of a wound. He said it had glanced off his ribcage.

'It was lucky I'd turned sideways,' he said to Emily. 'It winded me for a bit. But I'm all right now.'

They reached Reims, capital of the Champagne region, about forty-five minutes after leaving Paris and Benedict went to the café-bar to get something to eat.

When he'd gone Aunt Em subjected Jade to a piercing stare as if she'd done something wrong.

'What?' Jade said.

'It *winded* him. He took a bullet in the chest and it *winded* him.'

'Well . . . it glanced off his ribcage.'

'Oh, sure. What do you think they were firing – peas?'

Jade shrugged. 'Well, maybe he's wearing a bulletproof vest or something.'

'Yeah. Regulation issue for monks is it, these days?

Or maybe it bounced off his crucifix.' Jade said nothing. 'His shirt was soaked in blood. I saw it when we left the catacombs. He wouldn't let me examine him but I saw how much blood there was and believe me it was a serious wound. I know. I'm a doctor.'

'There's no blood now,' Jade pointed out.

'That's because he's changed his shirt. But why isn't he still bleeding?'

'Maybe he used a plaster.'

'Oh, give me a break. OK.' She raised her hands. 'If you don't want to tell me—'

'What can *I* tell you?' Jade demanded indignantly. 'How should *I* know why it's stopped bleeding.'

'I don't know. But something's going on. And you know more about it than you're cracking on.'

Benedict came back with a stack of smoked-salmon sandwiches and a bottle of chilled white wine.

'Gives you a hell of an appetite, getting shot,' he said.

Emily sniffed but she ate the sandwiches. She even had a glass or two of wine. They wouldn't let Jade have any. She had to have apple juice.

'But we're in Champagne,' she complained.

'No we're not. That was the last stop,' Benedict told her. 'We're almost on the Rhine.'

173

The shadows lengthened, the sun trailing in their wake. They left France behind and sped on through Germany. Rushing on through the darkness. Black fields and forests. Silver trails of rivers in the moonlight and ribbons of light flagging an autobahn or a small town. Villages flashing past like meteors in the night sky, burned out in a second. Frankfurt and Stuttgart came and went. Europe shrank before their rushing progress: the land that armies had tramped across and fought over for centuries, this way and that, east to west and back again, the fortified cities and the battlefields reduced to this, a fleeting glimpse through a train window. Jade didn't even see that much; she slept through most of it.

They reached Munich just after ten and Benedict rushed them off to a bar to buy beer and bratwurst before they caught the night train to Budapest.

'Nothing but the best for Friar Tuck,' remarked Aunt Em dryly as they made their way to the couchette.

Jade had the top bunk. She lay there staring at the ceiling. It bothered her that she hadn't told Aunt Em the whole story about Benedict — or at least as much as she herself knew. She lay there for several minutes thinking about it.

There was silence from the bottom bunk. It felt like a disapproving silence.

'Aunt Em?' she said tentatively.

'Yes?' It was a loaded yes. A dubious yes. A long-drawn-out distrustful yes.

'You know Benedict?'

'Do I know Benedict? Yes. Not as well as you do, obviously, but as well as I think I ever want to.'

'Well, the thing is – he's a bit . . . you know, weird.'

'You don't say.'

'Yes. I mean, *really* weird.'

'You mean as in stark, staring bonkers weird? Or just average weird?'

Aunt Em had a surprising vocabulary for a doctor.

'Well, what would you say if I told you he was seven hundred and eighty-five years old?'

No response.

'Aunt Em?'

'I'd say you were a few crumbs short of a bratwurst yourself, if you really want to know.'

'Well, that's what he told me. He said he was born in 1225 – in Transylvania.'

Silence.

'I know it sounds crazy. But it . . . well, it would explain the wound, wouldn't it?'

More silence.

'Aunt Em?'

'Why would it explain the wound?'

'Because . . . he can't die. I mean, not like ordinary people. If he gets hurt it heals. And he doesn't get sick and he doesn't age. Or at least, he doesn't age like the rest of us. And it's the same with Kobal.'

'What do you mean, *it's the same with Kobal*?'

'He's got the same thing. Because they're brothers. Twin brothers. Their mother was a Romanian gypsy who was burned as a witch.'

'Uh huh.'

'Yes. You think this is all drivel, don't you?'

'Drivel is one word for it. I can think of others. What else did he tell you?'

'Well, his father – *their* father – was a crusader. One of the Knights of Saint Saviour's. He was fighting in Transylvania at the time – for the King of Hungary – and he met their mother and fell in love. So they strangled him and drove a stake through his heart.'

'Because he fell in love?'

'Because she was a witch. A gypsy sorceress.'

'Oh, well then, that would explain it, of course. Probably a pioneer feminist, too.'

'They thought he'd come under her spell. And

she'd turned him into a vampire. One of the Undead. That's why they drove a stake through his heart. That's what you do with the Undead.'

'Thanks, I'll remember that if I ever come across one. I'm beginning to think Sister Sarah had a point.'

More silence, but Jade could tell she was still awake. She waited patiently. It was like when she was telling her vampire stories to the other kids at Saint Severa's. They might tell her to shut up but their curiosity always got the better of them.

'So what happened to the terrible twins?'

'They were brought up by monks. And they both entered the Order. But Boris — that's Kobal's real name — turned out bad and they expelled him.'

'And he can't be killed?'

'No. Well, not easily. Benedict says if you put a bomb under them they'd probably have a bit of a problem.'

'Oh, well, that's something, I suppose.'

'And of course there's all that stuff about silver bullets and stakes through the heart. And they can be killed by their own kind. Like, each other.'

'Benedict didn't think of this, then, when they were kids? Strangling him or driving a stake through his heart? As if in play.'

'No. I don't think so.'

'Pity.'

'They weren't brought up together. Kobal was brought up in Germany and Benedict in England.'

'Jade, let me tell you something . . .' Aunt Em's voice was serious now and Jade braced herself for a lecture, or worse. And it *was* worse. It was a kind of confession. 'I worked with Kobal. We were friends. Of sorts. In fact, I'll be honest with you, we were more than that . . .'

Jade winced. She felt like covering her ears. She wondered if she had always known this, in the back of her mind. But it wasn't something she cared to think about.

'He was very clever – too clever by half – but there was nothing superhuman about him, believe me. And another thing, we worked for the government. We worked on something that needed security clearance. At the highest level. Kobal was thoroughly vetted – more thoroughly than most given his background. He was born in Romania in 1968 when the country was ruled by a Communist dictator called Nicolae Ceauşescu. It was a particularly ugly, repressive regime. Kobal's father died in prison and his mother disappeared. He was brought up in an orphanage. He didn't have any brothers or sisters. When he was in his early teens he went on a camping holiday to Hungary, which was also Communist then, and while he was there he managed to escape over the border into Austria. He studied medicine at the University of Vienna and then in Rome. He became a brilliant geneticist with an international reputation. Then he came to work in England. That's the true story of Kobal. As I know it. So you can forget all these fantasies about being born in 1225, the son of a Romanian gypsy and a crusading vampire.'

Longish pause. Jade lay there, staring into the darkness, trying to make sense of all this.

'You do know it's ridiculous, don't you?' Emily persisted, and when Jade didn't answer . . . 'Jade?'

'Yes but . . . Benedict says it is, too. Ridiculous. But they're living proof, he says. He thinks it might be some kind of . . . of mutant gene.'

'A mutant gene?'

'Well, I think that's what he said.'

'Jade, I'm a geneticist. I know about genes. And believe me there is no gene, mutant or otherwise, that can make you live for ever. Or stop you bleeding if you get a bullet in the chest.'

'How did it happen then?'

'I don't know. I'm still working on it.'

'Well, let me know when you find out.' Jade could be every bit as scathing as Aunt Em if she put her mind to it.

'Do you think you've got this "mutant gene", then?'

'What do you mean?'

'Do you think *you* can live for ever?'

'No. I know I'm just the same as everyone else . . .' Jade would never have admitted that a few months ago. 'When I get hurt I bleed, like everyone else. I can get sick, like everyone else. And sooner or later I'm going to die, like everyone else.' She lay there staring into the dark.

'Jade?'

'Yes?'

'Give me your hand.'

Almost reluctantly, Jade reached out in the darkness.

'I'm sorry,' said Emily.

'What for? Because I'm going to die? It's not your fault.'

'No. Not because of that.'

But she didn't give any other reason.

'Benedict says it's not all that cool living for ever,'

said Jade after a while.

'Oh yeah?'

'He says there's no sense of . . . of completion. He says people have to move on. Only they have to die first.'

'I see. There was bound to be a catch. And when did you and Benedict have this little heart-to-heart?'

'In Lapland. When he rescued me from Kobal.'

'Well, it's a nice idea.'

'But you don't believe it.'

'I'm a scientist, Jade. He's a man of religion. We have a completely different approach to life. And death.'

A long silence as the train rushed on through the night. Then Jade said, 'What *are* genes?'

'It's a bit late for a biology lesson,' Emily complained. But then after a moment she sighed. 'OK. To put it very simply – a gene is the basic unit of heredity – something that's passed on from parent to child, like a kind of code that tells you what you are. Or not what you are, but . . . what kind of qualities or traits you're going to have as a person, like what colour eyes or hair – those are the most obvious *visible* traits . . . Others aren't so visible. Like your blood type or . . . or the tendency to catch certain diseases.'

'Or to read people's minds. And to put thoughts into their heads.'

'We-ell . . .'

'That's what my fa— what Kobal did, isn't it? Made babies that were like him. With the same evil powers.'

'I wouldn't say they were evil . . .'

'So why was it wrong – what he did?'

'Oh, Jade. How can I explain this? We're at the cutting edge of medical science here. We don't know how safe it is to interfere with the way plants are grown, let alone human beings. We could cause terrible mutations, things we can't control. So certain research is banned. For ethical and safety reasons. And that's why Kobal was stopped.'

'And put in a prison for mad people.'

'Well, we don't call them mad nowadays but . . . We thought he was deranged. Dangerously deranged.'

'But you let him make me. And the other kids.'

Another sigh in the darkness. 'We failed to stop him. Yes.'

'And now I'm like him.'

'Jade, you're not like him. You're not at all like him.'

Jade heard her get out of bed. She felt her standing next to her in the darkness, felt her breath on her face, her hand stroking her hair.

'Listen to me. People pass on certain traits to their offspring – but not everything. People never turn out exactly like their parents, even if they look a bit like them. But they're not clones. They find their own identity. Other people help – their parents, sometimes, brothers and sisters, friends, teachers . . . role models like footballers and film stars, the films they watch, the books they read – whatever – but they . . . they develop an identity of their own. That's the wonder of it. That's the magic. They become themselves.'

Jade was crying silently in the darkness, she could feel the tears on her cheeks.

'Jade. Don't cry. Why are you crying?'

'I don't know,' said Jade.

'You don't have to be like your parents. Not unless you want to. You certainly don't have to be like Kobal. You have a choice. You can be yourself. Do you believe me?'

'Yes. I think so.'

'Then why are you so upset?'

'I'm not really. I just . . .'

'What?'

'I just wish I knew who my mother was.'

There was silence in the darkness.

'I know,' said Aunt Em eventually. 'I know, babe.'

She leaned over and kissed her on the cheek, where the tears were, and then went back to bed.

18

The Land of Dracula

They arrived in Budapest just after seven in the morning and Benedict took them to one of the station cafés for what he called 'a typical Hungarian breakfast'. He did the ordering – in fluent Magyar – and as each dish arrived he told them the names. *Kolbász*, a Hungarian sausage, *májkrém*, or liver pâté, and *véres hurka*, a kind of black pudding made of pig's blood and lumps of fat; two different types of cheese: *disznósajt*, which was hard, and *körözött*, which was soft; served with a form of French toast called *bundáskenyér* and a stack of pancakes. Jade stared at the feast in amazement but refused everything except the pancakes with lemon and honey; Emily stuck to toast and jam while Benedict scoffed the lot, washed down with several mugs of scalding-hot coffee.

'Do you think someone shot him again in the night?' asked Emily when he'd left the table briefly to go to the loo.

'He has to keep his strength up,' said Jade. 'He's a warrior monk.'

'Well, he clearly doesn't believe in fasting,' Emily commented. 'Where does he put it all?'

When he came back he paid the bill and told them they'd better get a move on – they had a train to catch.

'What about Budapest?' asked Jade, looking around the station.

'What *about* Budapest?' Benedict repeated, clearly puzzled.

'Well, don't we get to see it?'

Benedict looked at his watch. 'No time,' he said. 'Maybe on the way back.'

'You mean we can't even go shopping?' Emily protested.

'What do you want to go shopping for?' he demanded.

'Well, some clothes would be nice. I don't know if you've noticed but I'm still dressed as a nun.'

'You look fine as a nun,' Benedict assured her.

'Don't you think?' he appealed to Jade.

'She'd look better if she took her hands out of her pockets,' Jade pointed out. 'And she doesn't walk like a nun. She swaggers about too much. And she shouldn't cross her legs when she's sitting down; it's not very nun-like.'

'Thank you,' said Emily after a moment. 'What a little cutie you are. Have you ever been kicked by a nun? I'm told it's a very moving experience.'

'Well, you can kick her all the way to Platform Eight,' said Benedict, 'because that's where the next train is waiting and it leaves in approximately ten minutes.'

So they saw even less of Budapest than they had of Paris – just the view from the train window as they set off on the next leg of their journey, to Cluj in Romania.

'Cluj?' said Jade, wrinkling up her nose as she tried to get her tongue round it. 'What kind of name is that?'

'A terrible name, I agree. It's from the Latin *clus* – meaning closed.'

'Closed to what?' enquired Emily suspiciously.

'Well, there's some debate about that. It might be because it was a fortress for much of its early history

– "closed" to the barbarians. Or it might be because it's "closed in" by mountains. The Hungarians called it Kolosvar. The Germans Klausenburg. But now it's Cluj. Or Cluj-Napoca to give it its full name.'

Emily was rather more interested in how long it would take to get there.

'Eight hours,' Benedict told her complacently.

She groaned.

'But there's a food bar if you'd like me to get you something to eat.'

They both groaned.

For the first few hours they travelled across rolling plains of farmland and forest with the occasional lake sparkling in the wintry sun, but shortly after they crossed the border into Romania the country became wilder and hillier and they caught a glimpse of taller mountains beyond.

'That,' said Benedict, leaning over Jade's shoulder, 'is Transylvania.'

'Where Dracula came from,' she murmured. It seemed a long time since she had sat in the Great Hall at Saint Severa's under the watchful eye of Sister Beatrice writing *I must not tell wicked lies* and *Why Vampires Have No Basis in Reality*. If she had only known then that within a few days she'd be on her way to Transylvania!

Benedict looked startled.

'What do you know about Dracula?' he demanded.

'More than is good for her,' Emily replied with a sigh.

'Everyone knows about Dracula,' said Jade. 'He was a vampire. One of the Undead.'

He looked at her in suspicion. 'Did Kobal tell you that?'

'No.' Now she was surprised. 'Why should he?'

'What else do you know about him?' he demanded.

'Well . . .' She frowned as she tried to remember what she'd read. 'He was a count. Count Dracula. And he came from Transylvania. And when he was alive, properly alive, he used to stick people on stakes. Up through their bottoms and out through their—'

'That will do,' said Emily sharply. 'I've had enough. All right?'

There was a sudden jolt that threw them about in their seats and the train began to lose speed.

'What's going on?' demanded Emily, looking alarmed.

A few minutes later the train came to a complete halt, apparently in the middle of nowhere. After they'd been there about ten minutes Benedict went off to try and find out what was happening.

'There's a problem with the engine,' he said, when he came back. 'We're going to try and limp into the next station.'

'And then what?' Emily wanted to know. But he just shrugged and said this was Romania; you had to take things as they came.

The train moved off again in a series of shuddering stops and starts, but after a short while they reached a small station with a sign that said *Huedin*. The conductor finally made an announcement.

'We're going to wait here until they send a replacement engine up the line from Cluj,' Benedict translated for them.

'How long will that take?' Emily demanded, but the only response was another philosophical shrug.

'I suggest we get out and stretch our legs,' he said.

It was almost dark now and cold. Aunt Em beat a hasty retreat back to the train but Benedict and Jade joined a queue at the station café where they bought coffee and *papanasi* – doughnuts filled with cottage cheese and jam.

'Tell me about Dracula,' Jade asked him, sinking her teeth into the doughnut so the jam dribbled down her chin. 'What's he got to do with Kobal?'

He regarded her carefully over his coffee. 'I didn't say he had anything to do with Kobal. What makes you think he has anything to do with Kobal?'

'Well – why did you ask me if Kobal had told me about him?'

'Because it's the kind of thing that would appeal to him, that's all.'

'I bet there's more to it than that,' she persisted. 'I bet it's because he's a vampire.'

'OK.' He sighed. 'It's probably better you know the whole story, so you know the danger you could be in. But let's go outside, on the platform. It doesn't seem likely but just in case anyone here speaks English.'

So Jade zipped her new jacket up to her chin and they walked up and down the chilly platform in the gathering dusk while he told her the story.

'Dracula's real name was Vlad,' he began, 'and—'

'I know that,' she interrupted. 'He—'

'Do you want me to tell you this story or not?'

'Sorry. Go on.'

'He was a prince of Transylvania, born in 1431, the youngest son of the ruler. And when he was only five years old he was enrolled into a society of knights called the Order of the Dragon – or, in his native tongue, *Drăcul*.'

Drăcul. Jade felt the hairs rise on the back of her neck. She had enjoyed scaring the girls of Saint Severa's with her own stories of vampirism but it was a bit different when you were actually here in Transylvania, ringed in by mountains with darkness falling.

'It was a branch of my own Order,' Benedict continued. 'Which has had many different names over the years and many different functions. But the purpose of the Draculae, as they called themselves, was to fight the Turks. And they brought in one of our own knights to train them. A man called Brother Boris. Boris Kobalski.'

'Kobal!' Jade exclaimed.

'How could it be Kobal?' Benedict demanded teasingly. 'This was nearly six hundred years ago.'

'OK. Whatever. So what happened then?'

'Well, within weeks of his arrival he was causing havoc . . .'

'Couldn't possibly be Kobal,' Jade agreed. She caught his eye. 'Sorry.'

'As I said, their purpose was to fight the Turks, but shortly after Kobal joined them they began to fight among themselves.'

'Surprise surprise,' muttered Jade.

'Vlad's father was assassinated by his own royal bodyguard, Vlad's brother was blinded by red-hot irons and buried alive, and Vlad himself was handed over to the Turks.'

'Nice one, Dad,' Jade commented bitterly.

'Vlad was a hostage for the rest of his youth but the Turks seem to have taken to him. By all accounts he was a handsome, decent sort of chap and he was raised in the Sultan's palace, almost like one of the family. In fact they sent him back in his early twenties as their puppet. And as soon as he was crowned, who should turn up but Kobal. Looking exactly the same as when Vlad had first seen him, almost twenty years before. He hadn't aged at all. So Vlad, being a simple sort of soul, became convinced he knew the secret of eternal youth – and he wanted a piece of it. He would do anything Kobal wanted. And under Kobal's influence he became a tyrant. He made war on his neighbours and on his own people. He had thousands of people tortured to death.'

'Like being impaled on spikes.'

'Being impaled on a spike was the least of your worries if Vlad got hold of you, with Kobal egging him on.'

'What else did he do?'

'Never mind. His cruelties were so great that before long everyone had turned against him and he was betrayed to the Turks. They cut off his head and pickled it in vinegar and honey and sent it round the country as proof that he was dead.'

'And was that when he turned into a vampire?'

'That's just a myth. A story to frighten people.'

'And what about Kobal?'

'He disappeared, as he usually does when he's done his worst – only to turn up in another time and place to do something similar.'

He stopped and turned her by the shoulders, gazing seriously into her face.

'That's what Kobal does. He promises people power – or the secret of eternal life, or whatever it is they truly desire, and he corrupts them. He makes them his creatures. He turns them from good to evil.'

'Is that what he's trying to do with us? His kids.'

'I don't know what he wants with you,' Benedict admitted. 'But one thing I'm sure of – it isn't to save the planet. Or the human race. Not unless he's had a complete change of character. Everything he's ever done has been designed to *corrupt* the human race; to make the world a worse place, not better. Almost as if he wants to prove to someone – me, the Church, God, maybe – that people are basically evil, or at least capable of committing the worst possible crimes. But why he should want kids of his own . . . ?' He shrugged helplessly.

'Maybe he wants us to be like him.'

No reply.

'Do you think we are like him? That I'm like him?'

'No.' He considered her carefully. 'No. Not at all. Do you?'

'I don't know. Sometimes . . .' She blurted it out: 'Sometimes I wonder if they're my own thoughts I'm having – or his.'

'I know what you mean,' he said. 'But, you know, when I was very young, people used to tell me the Devil would whisper evil thoughts in my ear and I had to recognize them for what they were and resist them.'

'Do you think Kobal's the Devil?'

'No.' He grinned ruefully. 'He's my brother, so what would that make me?' Then after a moment he added, 'I'm not even sure if the Devil exists. At least, not as an individual. More like, he's a symbol of the dark side of human nature. And Kobal is certainly that.'

There was a sudden flurry of activity along the platform and they saw the headlights of a locomotive bearing down on them from the darkness to the east.

'The replacement engine,' said Benedict.

They watched as it was hitched to the front of their train.

'Better get back on before it goes without us,' he said. 'Or your Aunt Em will be starting to panic.'

But when they returned to their seats there was no sign of her – and soon it was Jade who started to panic.

'Stay there,' Benedict commanded her. 'I'll go and look for her. She's got to be somewhere on the train.'

He was still gone when they started to move out of the station.

Jade sat alone, fighting her fears. She peered out of the window, shielding her eyes against the reflections. There was nothing out there. Nothing but black night.

A few minutes later Benedict was back. Alone.

'I've gone the whole length of the train both ways,' he said, shaking his head. 'I even checked the toilets. I can't find her.'

'But – where can she be?'

'I don't know,' he said, 'but she's not on the train.'

19

The Missing Nun

They stood by the ticket barrier at Cluj and watched the other passengers filing past. Emily was not among them.

'Now what?' demanded Jade miserably. But for once Benedict seemed to be at a loss.

'We'll have to go to the police,' said Jade.

'And tell them what? That we're missing a nun. I'm sorry, I'll put that another way – we're missing someone *pretending* to be a nun. And what do we tell them about *you*?'

'You don't have to tell them anything about me. You could say you were travelling alone.'

'Just me and the nun.'

'Right.' She had an inspired thought. 'You could

say you were running away to get married. And . . . and you lost her.'

'Brilliant,' he said. 'No wonder Kobal wants you back. I don't know how he's coping without you.'

'Well . . . I don't hear any better ideas.'

'That's because I like to think before I speak.'

'Oh, good. Well, carry on, Sherlock. I'll just sit here till you're ready.'

She threw herself down on a station seat and folded her arms, feeling secretly quite pleased with herself because it was like something her Aunt Em might have said. But then of course she just felt worse because her Aunt Em *hadn't* said it. And they didn't have the faintest idea where she was.

'Well, there's no point in hanging round here,' said Benedict after a moment. 'We might as well find a hotel.'

'What if she comes in on the next train?'

'There isn't a next train. Not until tomorrow.'

Jade hated to leave the station. It seemed like the last link they had with her. But Benedict was right. They couldn't hang around the station all night; she could already feel the chill.

They booked in at the Hotel Transylvania in the

centre of Cluj. Jade waited for Benedict to order a large meal but for once he didn't seem to be hungry. Either that or he was too ashamed to admit it. They ordered drinks, instead, in the hotel bar.

'Have you had time to think yet?' she asked him.

'I have,' he said. 'And there are a number of possibilities.' He ticked them off on his fingers. 'One: she sneaked off the train at Huedin and hid.'

Jade stared at him in frank astonishment. 'Why would she do that?'

'She might have had enough of us.'

'She might have had enough of you,' Jade agreed, 'but she'd never have left me in the middle of Transylvania.'

'No. Probably not. OK – two: she went shopping for clothes and the train left before she had time to get back.'

Jade stared at him. 'Excuse me?'

'Well – she didn't like being a nun.'

This was true.

'She'd never have done that,' Jade protested. 'Anyway, there were no shops.'

'And she didn't have any money,' Benedict remembered. 'No money, no credit cards, no nothing.'

'So, no shopping.'

'No. So, three: someone snatched her off the train.'

'That's what I figured,' said Jade, 'as soon as she went missing.'

'Well, good for you. And did you figure how they managed to do this in full view of about two hundred passengers without anyone noticing or making a fuss?'

'Well, I've been thinking about that, and whoever did it could have told her I wasn't feeling very well. And taken her off to a quiet part of the station and then jumped her.'

'Ye-es . . .' He eyed her thoughtfully. 'I suppose that's possible. So the next question is – who jumped her and why?'

'Well, that's obvious. Kobal.'

'So did he follow us from England without us noticing – or was he there ahead of us, waiting for the train to break down at Huedin?'

'I don't know. But who else could it have been?'

'I suppose it could have been some of his people,' Benedict conceded, 'even if it wasn't Kobal himself. So we're left with the next question: why?'

'To hold her hostage,' said Jade. 'And swap her for me.'

'That's good,' he said, looking at her in surprise.

'Just a hunch,' she admitted modestly.

'I don't suppose you've got a hunch as to what they've done with her?'

'No. But if it *is* Kobal – or his people – we'll probably hear from them soon enough.'

'Well, now we've got that worked out . . .' he looked at his watch . . . 'I guess we'd better order dinner before they close the kitchens.'

Jade spent a restless night dreaming she was still on the train, searching for Aunt Em. She'd see someone who looked like her and she'd rush up only to find it was Kobal or Barmella dressed as a nun. And then it would turn into the old dream she'd had at Saint Severa's of being in a ruined castle and she'd wake up in a sweat. But at some stage she must have drifted into a deep sleep because she was jerked awake by the bedside phone. It was Benedict.

'Have you heard anything?' she asked. It was still dark.

'No.' He sounded surprised.

'So why did you phone me?'

'It's seven o'clock,' he said. 'Time for breakfast.'

It was a light breakfast by Benedict's standards. A

cheese omelette with cucumber and tomatoes and a pot of black tea.

'I've been thinking,' he began.

'That's good,' she encouraged him.

'I've been trying to think like Kobal.'

'Not so good.'

'Will you shut up for a minute?'

She sniffed.

'OK, let's just say he did follow us from London – what is he going to be thinking we're up to?'

She waited for him to tell her, but he seemed to be waiting on her.

The silence stretched.

'You want me to speak now?'

'Please.'

'Well, he's going to be thinking that we're trying to find this kid. The Child of the Spirit.'

'Exactly. And he's going to be hoping we'll lead him to wherever the boy is. I mean, he'd probably figure that this would be considerably easier than trying to make you do it for him.' This was true. 'So if you're right – and he's taken Emily hostage to exchange for you – he won't want to do that until we've found the other kid. Right?'

'You want me to speak again?'

He closed his eyes for a moment. He seemed to be under some considerable strain. 'Yes, please.'

'I think it sounds a good idea.'

'Excellent.' He clapped his hands.

'But what do we do then? When we find him and Kobal pops up and says, "Ah ha!"'

'Ah ha?'

'Or something like that. Like the Heffalump.'

'The Heffalump? I'm sorry, you've lost me.'

'Like in *Winnie the Pooh*.' She watched his face. 'Never mind. What will you do when he pops up with Aunt Em and says, "OK, guys, where's the dosh?"'

'The dosh?'

'Sorry. I was getting carried away. "OK guys, I've got the girl. Now hand over the rug-rats."'

'Rug-rats?'

'Brats.'

He stared at her in total bemusement.

'Will you fight him?' she persisted.

'I suppose so. If I must.'

'OK. You're on. Good idea.'

He shook his head. 'So we press on. As planned.'

'As planned.' She agreed. But then she frowned. 'What *have* we planned? I don't think you mentioned it.'

'Did I not?'

'Not as far as I remember.'

'Right. Well, we're going to drive to Bistrita, where this monastery used to be, and then we're going to drive up into the mountains and see if we can find it again.'

'Again?'

'Like you did the last time, in your imagination.'

'But I didn't find it. I kept getting lost. It was like he knew I was searching for him, in my mind, and he just kept me going round in circles. I think he's more powerful than me. I think he's more powerful than any of us. And if he doesn't want to be found, then no one's going to find him.'

'I know,' he said gently because he could see she was a bit distressed. 'But this time, now we're so close, maybe you'll have more luck. Maybe this time he'll want you to find him, now Kobal isn't with you, reading your mind.'

'Maybe.' But she wasn't convinced. 'I mean, it could have been anywhere. How do you know we're anywhere near the place?'

'Because I've been there. And so has Kobal. A long time ago. It was the place where we were born.'

20

The Lost Monastery

Jade gazed from the side window of the SUV as they drove up into the mountains. Benedict had hired a four-wheel drive 'in case we need to go off the beaten track' but from what Jade could see a helicopter would have been more useful. Certainly she could see few tracks, beaten or otherwise, in the rugged terrain that greeted her brooding inspection. The Carpathians. Largest mountain range in Europe, Benedict had told her, stretching up from the Balkans through Romania to Poland and the Ukraine . . . Haunt of the grey wolf and the brown bear, the chamois and the lynx and the eagle. And other more sinister creatures, if you could believe the folk tales . . .

'Why can't you find it, if you were born there?' She frowned, voicing a question she had been nursing since they left the hotel.

'I don't know what it was like for you when *you* were born but personally I wasn't taking much notice of my surroundings at the time,' he explained. 'Too busy screaming I expect. And a few days later they moved us to Klausenberg for the *auto-de-fé*.'

'What's an *auto-de-fé*?'

'Literally – it means an act of faith. But in the past, it involved burning somebody at the stake. Burning them alive. A heretic or a witch usually. In this case, my mother.'

'I'm sorry,' she said. Then, after a moment: 'We didn't have much luck with our mothers, did we?'

He glanced sideways at her.

'You make your own luck,' he said. 'For good or ill.'

'Do you really believe that?'

'I do. Well – you hope for a little help from your friends from time to time.'

She returned to the matter in hand. 'Still, it was a long time ago – what makes you think this place is still there?'

'I don't. It's just a hunch.'

'And it's called the Monastery of the Holy Spirit?'

'Or the Holy Ghost. It's the same thing.'

'If it still existed you'd have found it on the internet,' she pointed out. He'd checked the internet when he was in London. They'd even checked in the phone book at Cluj and it wasn't listed.

'It doesn't exist,' he said. 'It's a ghost.'

'Ha ha.'

'I'm serious. It has to be a ghost. Or behave like one. It's the only way for it to evade its enemies. First there were the Turks, then the Communists. And of course, always there was Kobal. It had to keep its head down. Keep moving around. Now you see me, now you don't.'

'It's a building,' she pointed out. 'How do you hide a building?'

'Well, first you build it somewhere very remote. Then, when you think people are closing in on you, you move out and build another one somewhere else. But I have a feeling the original one is still there. Even if it's a ruin.'

'If it's a ruin, how could the kid be there?'

'I don't know that either. But sometimes you just have to follow your instincts.'

So they followed the long, winding road up into

the mountains and after a few more miles it began to descend, dropping steeply into a wooded valley where they saw the first signs of human life. Small houses just off the road, painted in bright colours: blues and reds and greens . . . And the occasional cultivated field. Cows and horses. Geese in a meadow. Then, in the distance, the roofs of a large town.

'Bistrita,' Benedict announced. 'Capital of Dracula country.'

'I thought you said there was no such thing as Dracula.'

'I didn't say that at all. Don't you ever listen? I said he wasn't a vampire. But he *was* a real person. Vlad Tepes, Knight of the Order of the Dragon.'

'And this is where he lived?'

'He lived in many places. But he's believed to have had a castle somewhere in the mountains east of the town.'

Whatever dragons or demons it had nurtured in the past, Bistrita appeared to be cleansed of them now: it looked a pretty, prosperous-looking place of red-roofed buildings and neat, cobbled streets and squares. It had been built by Saxon settlers in the fourteenth century, Benedict told her, and indeed it looked like pictures Jade had seen of an old-fashioned town in Germany, a town out of a fairy tale.

'Don't let it fool you,' Benedict warned her. 'This place is steeped in blood and violence. It would turn your stomach if you knew half the things that have happened here.'

This didn't stop him from taking her to the Golden Krone hotel in the centre of town and ordering a traditional lunch of 'robber steak', which turned out to be bits of bacon, beef and onions threaded on a stick and heavily laced with paprika. Jade had no appetite – she was too worried about Aunt Em – but Benedict urged her to eat something, just to keep her strength up.

'You never know where your next meal might come from,' he told her cheerfully. 'Besides, you need to feed that brain of yours, keep it active. In case he tries to reach you.'

'In case who tries to reach me?'

'The boy.'

'You think he will?'

'I think he might.'

'How do you mean "reach me"?'

'Communicate with you. Through the mind.'

She nibbled dutifully at a bit of a kebab.

'How do you think it works,' she asked him,

'this mind thing?'

'*This mind thing?*'

'You know, picking up people's thoughts.'

'How do *you* think it works?'

She shrugged but then after a moment she said, 'It's like you suddenly get a signal. Like a radio message. Or a TV signal, 'cos sometimes it's a picture. It just turns up in your head and you don't know where it comes from.'

'And what about when *you* send a signal?'

'I'm not supposed to do that,' she replied cautiously.

'But you have, haven't you?' He eyed her shrewdly.

'You mean – recently?' She played for time.

'Recently enough to remember what it's like.'

How could he know what she'd done to Rose and Jasmine? But he knew. She could tell by his face that he knew.

'Well, it's like you kind of picture something in your head and you . . . *think* it at someone. And sometimes it works and sometimes it doesn't. And it usually gives me a headache. And Aunt Em says I shouldn't do it and it will only get me in trouble,' she finished, staring down at her plate and fighting back the tears.

'We'll find her,' he said, placing a hand over hers. 'But I think maybe first we have to find the boy – and that rather depends on you.'

'Why not you?' She looked up at him challengingly. 'You can do the same thing. Better than I can.'

'Not in this case,' he told her quietly. 'I don't know why, but I can't. And nor can Kobal.'

'I haven't had that much luck myself,' she said. 'Not with this kid.'

He watched her carefully.

'Perhaps you're losing your powers,' he said.

'Does that happen?'

'It can do. If you don't use them much. Also, maybe you can grow out of them.'

'How do you mean, "grow out of them"?'

'Like you grow out of lots of things. You put aside childish things.'

'Is it childish?'

'It might be linked to the imagination, which is stronger in children.'

'You haven't grown out of it,' she pointed out.

'No. That's true. Maybe I haven't grown up yet.'

'I wouldn't mind if I did grow out of it, the trouble it's given me.'

'Do you mean that?'

She wondered if she did. 'I used to think it would be great to be different,' she said. 'To have some special kind of power, like magic. But now, I don't know. Sometimes I'd just like to be ordinary. If only people would leave me alone.'

'I know the feeling,' he remarked dryly. 'But while Kobal's around, it isn't going to happen.'

They ate in silence for a while. Then he said, 'Tell me about the other kids. The ones he brought to the castle in Lapland.'

She shrugged. 'What about them?'

'Did they have any special powers?'

'You mean, to read people's minds? I'm not sure. It's not something we ever talked about. I don't think any of them could put thoughts in my head. But it's hard to know.'

'Did you like them? Did you have much in common?'

She thought about it. 'Not really. I didn't know them that well. We weren't like proper brothers and sisters and we weren't together long. The only thing, you know, we had in common was that Kobal was our father. Or at least he said he was. But we didn't grow up together and we all had different mothers.'

'And were any of you like *him*?'

'Not really. Maybe a bit. I worried that I was. Maybe I am.'

She looked to him for reassurance but all he said was: 'What else?'

She sighed. 'Well, I suppose Paco was the one I knew best. He was the one I rescued from the dump in Guatemala. Wish I'd left him there,' she added fiercely.

'Why?'

'Because . . . oh, he was a little rat. He was the most like Kobal, I think. Except that he was so kind of . . . thin and scrawny. But he was mean, you know? You could see it in his eyes. Mean and always, like, looking for a weakness. You could feel him, searching for it. Maybe he was trying to put thoughts in my head, now I think about it – but it wasn't like thoughts, it was more . . . like he was trying to burn you up. To turn your brain to mush. That's what he did to the others, I think.'

'You think Kobal would have let him?'

'I don't know. Maybe not. He was Kobal's favourite.' She blushed. 'After I let him down.'

'By not finding the seventh child?'

'That – and other things.'

'So, you didn't like Paco. What about the others?'

'Well, there was Shrika, the one from India. She was the Child of Magic. She'd been to the School of Magic in Kerala, in India, and when I found her she was working in a circus. I think she had power over animals. I mean, she could, like, read their thoughts and maybe she could *give* them thoughts, too. I mean, like, put thoughts in their heads. She could make them do anything she wanted. Maybe she could do it with people, too, I don't know. I don't think she was very interested in people. She was very beautiful,' Jade added as an afterthought. She was talking about them as if they were dead, she reflected. Maybe they were.

'And the other three?' he prompted her gently.

'Oh, I didn't know them at all. They'd only just turned up before it went all nasty and I ran away. There was Kai. She was the Child of the Sea. From one of the islands in the Pacific. She was quite shy. She didn't really want to know anyone. Didn't want to know me, anyway. But I was – I mean, it was obvious Kobal had it in for me, by then, and she probably didn't want to make trouble for herself. I thought she was kind of . . . I mean she'd go along with whoever seemed to be, you know, the strongest and the most useful to her. Like Paco. He was the gang leader. And Kobal encouraged him.'

Benedict nodded as if he understood.

'Then there was Solomon. He came from the mountains of the Moon in Uganda but he was . . . I think he'd been in some kind of rebel army, what they called a boy soldier. He'd been taken from his family – I mean his mother, his host mother – and he was forced to join a gang of rebels fighting in the bush. I think he was scared and bullied and he'd done some bad things, terrible things, but he didn't talk about them.'

'Then how did you know?'

'I suppose . . . I must have picked up his thoughts . . . But not deliberately. He didn't speak much English. So he hardly spoke at all. And he just followed Paco, around, like a dog. I know I shouldn't say that. But he was like one of the gang Paco had on the dump in Guatemala City.

'And then there was Barega. I liked him the best. At least I didn't *dislike* him. He came from Australia, somewhere in the north, on the coast. He was the Child of the Wind.'

'Why was that?'

'Why the Wind? I don't know. Maybe because it was so windy there.'

'There wasn't a shrine, to the god of the wind? A place of sacrifice.'

'I don't know. I mean he didn't say. It wouldn't surprise me, though. Why do you ask?'

'Because most of these places seem to be linked with sacrifice of some sort. Human sacrifice.'

This was true in her case, too. She had been born on the site of an old Druid temple in the Forest of Windsor, where the ancient Druids who had ruled England before the Romans used to sacrifice people to the gods of the trees. They used to hang human heads in trees. Gross.

'And why do you think the others stay with him?' he asked her. 'Why haven't they tried to escape, like you?'

'I don't know. Maybe they're too scared. And some of them probably reckon he's going to reward them in some way. He was always going on about what we could do together. And how he'd show us how we could use our powers. But he never did.' She brooded on this for a moment. Then she said, 'I wish I knew why he's doing this. I mean, why did he have us in the first place?'

'I don't know. If I knew that I'd be close to knowing how his mind works. And I don't. Maybe he just wanted to have children. Seven perfect children.'

'Are we perfect?'

'Well, I don't know about the others,' he said, 'but as far as you're concerned I've seen a lot worse.'

'So you don't think I'm like him?'

'I don't think you're at all like him.'

They finished their meal in silence and then headed back to the car and followed the road east, up into the mountains again, into the heart of Dracula country, for this was the Burgo Pass, where Vlad's castle was supposed to lie hidden, among the lofty pinnacles of rock and the deep forested valleys. Higher and higher they climbed as the sun fell swiftly behind them, climbing into a rocky wilderness that seemed strangely raw and unfinished to Jade, as if a giant sculptor had set about it with hammer and chisel and then got fed up and walked away, leaving it in the first disorderly stages of creation. Or maybe he'd achieved exactly what he intended: a monument to Chaos. The flayed mountain flanks rose high above them, scoured by jagged rifts and fissures. Soaring crags thrust their ugly features to the sky like Frankenstein monsters screaming to be made whole, or put out of their misery. Massive boulders leaned this way and that and sometimes upon each other like drunken trolls locked in battle or an embrace. Here a landslide had swept through a straggling forest and the broken trees lay like amputated limbs in a squalor of fallen rock. There a waterfall plunged in angry confusion, seeking gentler pastures. And the twisting, turning road climbed ever upward, seeking its own salvation, threading through the needle's eye of countless tunnels, hugging impossible slopes, skirting deep and deadly chasms clothed in shadow. No sign of human life. Once a circling eagle, high above a crag. Once a dead thing, draped upon a rock far below, a feast for crows and vultures. The sun sank, the clouds pressed in upon them and soon it began to rain, and as they climbed higher the rain changed to sleet and the sleet to a brittle, flinty snow.

They reached the head of the pass and the road suddenly ran straight for at least a mile across a bleak, empty plateau. And Jade felt ill.

'Stop the car,' she groaned. Benedict took one look at her ashen face and pulled into the side of the road.

She groped for the door handle and stumbled out into the biting cold. But almost as soon as she left the car the nausea passed and she looked up and gazed around her and she had a strange feeling that she had been here before.

And then through the swirling snow and the fleeting cloud she saw it – just for an instant before the clouds closed in again – and she looked at Benedict, who was hovering over her, his eyes filled with concern, and for a moment she thought she would not tell him and that she would let him drive on, away from this place and whatever future it held for her.

But of course she could not do that.

'This is it,' she told him. 'This is the place.'

And then another ragged gap opened in the clouds and she saw it again, high on its lofty perch above the road. The lost monastery. The place of the spirit.

21

Wolf!

There was a road — of sorts. A rough track winding down through the valley and they could see it continuing up the far side until it was lost in the trees. It looked more suited to a mountain goat than a motor vehicle but Benedict took the SUV down there, jolting and lurching over the many ruts and boulders and easing it gingerly round the bends with Jade gripping the dash with both hands, despite her seatbelt, and moaning quietly whenever they veered too close to the edge. Not quietly enough, apparently.

'Do you have to make that noise?' Benedict demanded.

'Sorry,' she said. 'It helps me concentrate.'

'Well, it doesn't help me,' he pointed out. 'And I'm

the one who needs to concentrate.'

At least it had stopped snowing, though the clouds held the promise of more. The sun had dropped behind the mountains and they were in deep shadow. Jade consulted her watch. It was just after four o'clock. They would never get back, she thought, in the dark.

There was a river at the bottom of the valley, a torrent of white water hurtling through rocks – but there was also a bridge: a stone bridge that looked as if it had been there for centuries, though Jade had serious doubts about it being here much longer if Benedict tried to drive the SUV over it.

'Do you think it's safe?' she ventured. She had no desire to repeat her experience in Cumbria.

'You can get out and walk if you like,' Benedict offered, 'and I'll wait for you on the other side.'

Jade seriously considered it. But if Benedict went down with the bridge she'd be stranded alone in the middle of the Burgo Pass with night coming on.

'I'll stay with you,' she said, closing her eyes.

She swore she could feel the bridge tremble when they drove on to it and several large stones broke away and fell into the river. But it held together long enough for them to reach the other side.

Now they faced the next test: a daunting climb up the far side of the valley along a track that appeared even rougher and narrower than the one that had brought them down. It was deeply rutted by rainwater that poured from the slopes above and so eroded in parts their wheels were just centimetres from the edge. Benedict was forced to make frequent stops to remove rocks that had fallen into the road, some of them the size of a football, but then, after they had been climbing for almost an hour, he finally met his match: a massive landslide that had buried the track under tons of rock.

Benedict switched off the engine. A sudden silence broken only by a sound like cracking ice from under the bonnet. He closed his eyes and put his head on the wheel. Jade wondered if he was praying.

'What now?' she said.

Benedict raised his head. 'Well, we can back up until we find somewhere to turn,' he said, 'or we can sit here until they send someone to mend the road – which might, or might not happen, sometime in the next thousand years. Or we can get out and walk.'

They got out and walked.

Fortunately, during their brief stay in Cluj, he had bought walking boots and anoraks for them both and filled a rucksack with some provisions and basic equipment including a rope and a torch. But first there was the small matter of the landslide.

Benedict inspected it from below.

'I'd better go first,' he said, 'and we'll rope you up in case you fall.'

He looped the rope under her arms and left her standing at the bottom while he began to climb, testing each rock carefully before putting his weight on it. When he reached the top he braced himself as securely as he could, took the rope firmly in both hands and signalled her to begin her own assent.

At first it seemed quite easy. Much easier than the climb above the river in Cumbria. There were plenty of handholds and the rocks appeared to be firmly embedded in the shale. Benedict let her do the work, drawing in the slack as she climbed towards him. Within a few minutes she was standing next to him at the top. They could see the track winding up the mountain on the other side.

'OK,' he said. 'Wait here until I'm down.'

She gazed down into the valley. It was in deep shadow but she could just make out the glint of white water far below. She felt like a god, or an eagle in its mountain eyrie. Two steps and she could be soaring into the valley. It was a terrible temptation. Her feet began to move towards the edge almost of their own volition.

'OK, put the rope back on.' Benedict had reached the track on the other side. Jade snapped out of her deadly trance and raised the loop of rope to slip over her head – and in that instant a stone turned under her foot and she fell.

She grabbed at a rock to steady herself but it came away in her hand and then the whole pack moved under her and she was sliding towards the edge of the landslide in another small avalanche of loose rock and shale.

But she still held the rope. And in the last instant before she went over the edge it hooked on a projecting rock. The loop tightened around her wrist and she hung there, with the lower half of her body dangling over the cliff and a cascade of stones tumbling past her and spinning down into the valley below.

Benedict was already scrambling up to where the rope had snagged. He seized it in both hands and braced himself.

'Hang on!' he shouted. 'Whatever you do, don't let go. I'm going to haul you up.'

She could do little else but hang on. The rope had looped tightly around her wrist. She could feel it biting into the flesh. She reached up with her other hand and grasped the rope just above the loop.

'Ready?'

'Ready,' she called back, gritting her teeth against the pain.

And slowly he began to haul her in.

'It could have been worse.' Benedict eased the rope from her tortured wrist. 'It could have been your neck.'

They scrambled down to the track and Benedict made her sit down on a rock while he wiped the dirt from her face and bandaged up her wrist where the rope had bitten into the skin.

Then they began the next climb.

They had need of the torch now for night fell rapidly in the mountains and the forest pressed in either side. Jade tried not to think of the dangers it might conceal. Brown bear and grey wolf, lynx and wild boar did not worry her anything like as much as the other creatures she had read about: the creatures that had made the Burgo Pass feared by travellers for centuries, though Benedict derided them as creatures of myth and superstition, fantasy figures from the pages of fairy tales.

Even so, Jade felt watched by hidden eyes and at times she imagined she could hear the pad of some large beast tracking them through the trees. But when she mentioned this to Benedict he said it was 'probably the wind'.

'I told you, there is no such thing as vampires,' he said. 'Dracula was no more a vampire than I am.'

'You were born nearly eight hundred years ago,' Jade pointed out.

'Point taken, but I don't have fangs. I don't live in a coffin. I don't come out at night and suck blood from the living. However, if we don't find this monastery of yours soon I might be tempted.'

And so they tramped on up the endless track, following the wavering beam of the torch as the darkness closed in around them. It began to snow again, more heavily now, settling on trees and track. Jade hadn't yet begun to feel the cold – she was actually sweating from the climb – but she dreaded the thought of spending the night on the open mountain. But then suddenly the moon emerged through a gap in the clouds and they saw the dark but oddly familiar shape on a pinnacle of rock above the track – with a tall bell tower outlined against the night sky.

There were steps cut into the rock – a lot of steps. It took all of Jade's remaining energy to drag herself up but, after several pauses for her to catch her breath in the thin mountain air, they finally reached the top. And there it was. Whatever it was. Smaller than Jade's impression when she had first seen it, in her imagination: more hermitage than monastery, with a wooden cross above the door and a light in one window high above.

There was an old-fashioned bell pull beside the door. Benedict pulled it. A distant chime sounded from within. But no immediate response. He was about to try again when a panel slid open in the door and two dark eyes peered out at them. Benedict said something in what was presumably the local tongue and a lengthy dialogue ensued while Jade stamped her feet in the snow and blew steam into the air. At last she heard the sound of bolts being pulled back and with an ominous creak the door swung open.

Benedict pushed her ahead of him across the threshold where she was confronted by a tall, bearded man in a black robe and a tall, black hat. He looked very old.

'This is Brother Gavril,' said Benedict. 'Say hello.'

'Hello,' said Jade obligingly.

'*Boo-nuh-see-wah*,' said Brother Gavril, or at least that's what it sounded like. His mouth contained a pair of broken teeth roughly the shape of some of the crags they'd seen on the way up through the Burgo Pass.

He reached into an alcove above his head and produced a stub of candle in a pewter holder. Then, shielding the guttering flame with one hand, he led them along a narrow corridor and up a flight of stone stairs.

'Where's he taking us?' Jade whispered.

'To see the hegemen,' Benedict said unhelpfully.

Brother Gavril led them along another corridor and paused outside a closed door. He said something to Benedict, knocked and then opened the door a fraction and slid his wiry frame through the gap.

'He wants us to wait,' said Benedict.

They waited.

'What's a hegemen?' asked Jade.

'A hegemen is the name for an abbot in the Romanian Orthodox Church.'

'I thought so,' she said. She looked about her. 'Is this where you were born?'

'I told you,' he said, 'I have no memory of it.' But then he said, 'I think it probably was.'

'How do you feel?' she asked him gently.

Benedict sighed. 'Strange,' he said.

The door opened and Brother Gavril's head appeared in the crack. He spoke one word.

'The hegemen has agreed to an interview,' Benedict said. 'Be very polite.'

'I'm always polite,' Jade retorted. 'After you.'

He levered her into the room with a firm hand in the small of her back.

The room was dimly lit by several candles and a wood-burning stove that appeared to produce more smoke than heat. So much smoke that at first Jade thought the room was empty but then she saw the figure seated by the casement window. He was dressed much the same as Brother Gavril but seemed even more ancient and Jade could tell from the length of his beard that he was infinitely more important.

'I have been watching your approach for the past hour or more,' he said in surprisingly good English. 'I was wondering who it might be. We do not receive many visitors in the Monastery of the Holy Spirit.'

So at least they had come to the right place.

'However, you are welcome to our meagre hospitality,' the hegemen continued, extending his hands towards them in a blessing. Cue for Brother

Gavril to serve the drinks – though from the look of the dark, viscous liquid he poured into three earthenware mugs it wasn't going to be happy hour.

Benedict had started talking Romanian again. The hegemen began to frown and shot several searching glances at Jade. Finally he spoke to her directly in his rasping English.

'So you search for your lost brother?' he said. 'The brother you never see. Well, that is sad. Very sad. But I am sorry I cannot help you. Your brother is not here. There is no child here. No. Not any more. Only old men.'

It was true that the monastery had formerly been in Bistrita, Benedict explained. The monks had run a small school and orphanage there but some five or six years ago, desiring a more contemplative life, they had removed themselves to this remote mountain retreat.

'It is over eight hundred years old,' the hegemen informed Jade proudly, 'but then we move to Bistrita and for most of the last century it is empty. A place of bats and owls and other creatures not so harmless. However . . . ' he indicated the crumbling walls '. . . as you see, we make it good. Good for us to live in. We bring some small comforts. Even some part of the modern world.'

Jade wondered what part. She sipped cautiously from the cup Brother Gavril had given her and almost choked. It tasted like the vilest kind of cough medicine.

'This boy,' Benedict persisted, speaking English now, presumably for Jade's benefit, 'could he have been among those taken into the orphanage when it was in Bistrita?'

'I will send for the records,' the hegemen said, 'but we had stopped taking orphans long before the time of which you speak. I am afraid you have had a wasted journey,' he informed Jade gently.

Suddenly from the darkness beyond the window came a sound that made the hairs rise on the back of Jade's neck.

The mournful howl of a wolf.

The effect on the hegemen was dramatic. The cup he was holding dropped from his fingers and shattered in a dozen pieces on the stone floor. The spilled liquid spread in a dark pool at his feet.

Jade started in surprise, for scary though it was, it cannot have been the first time the old man had heard the howl of a wolf. Not in the region of the Burgo Pass.

And yet there was fear in his eyes and his hands

shook as he made a helpless gesture towards the mess on the floor.

Another howl. It seemed to be coming from directly beneath the window and Jade had to stop herself from running forward and peering out. The hegemen shot a look at Brother Gavril, who hurried from the room. Jade bent to pick up the shards of pottery from the floor. Benedict restrained her with a hand.

'You are much troubled by wolves, Reverend Father?'

The hegemen made an attempt to recover his dignity but his eye strayed nervously to the window. He smiled shakily at Jade. 'It is an ancient fear, is it not, the terror of the wolf.'

There was another sound. More of a growl than a howl and it sounded closer, almost as if it was inside the confines of the monastery itself. The hegemen sat tense in his chair, gazing past them towards the door. Suddenly it flew wide open, the candles were extinguished by a blast of cold air, and a dark shape bounded into the room and crouched panting before them.

But it was not a wolf. Jade would have been less astonished if it were.

And in the silence, broken only by the harsh breathing of the creature on the floor, Benedict spoke.

'Hello, boy,' he said. 'May I introduce you to your sister, Jade.'

22

Angel

A match flared in the darkness as Brother Gavril relit the smouldering candles and with a soft growl the creature retreated into the shadows on the far side of the room. But its eyes were fixed on Jade and not for a moment did it relieve her of its intense inspection, even when Brother Gavril shook his fist at it and muttered what was clearly a scathing rebuke before shuffling, still grumbling, from the room.

'I am sorry to deceive you,' said the hegemen with a sigh, 'but perhaps you understand now why it is so. Sometimes I do not know if he is wolf or boy – and I do not know if he does . . .' He smiled gently at the beast. 'But he is still our Inger, our little angel of the woods, and for all his foolishness, he is under our protection.'

'Inger?' Benedict looked sharply at him.

'In the English, it means Angel.'

'I know that. But who called him that? Your people?'

'No. He was called that when he came to us. Is it important?'

As the light of the candles crept into the corners of the room Jade saw that he was, in fact, far more boy than wolf, at least in appearance. He wore a pair of leather trousers hacked off at the knee and a shaggy coat that might have been sheep or goatskin: it was difficult to tell, it was so filthy and matted. His long hair hung down below his shoulders, his feet were bare, and Jade could see a network of scars through the dirt on his arms and legs. And yet there was a extraordinary, almost delicate beauty about his features. He put her in mind of Mowgli, of course, the wolf boy in *The Jungle Book*. He even had a knife, as Mowgli had, in a scabbard hanging from a string around his neck. But there was something else about him that eluded her for the moment. He was between ten and twelve years old, she judged; it was impossible to be more precise.

Benedict spoke to him in the same tongue he had used to address the monks but though the dark eyes flickered briefly in his direction there was no response beyond another soft growl.

'He cannot understand you, my son,' said the hegemen. 'Nor can he speak, in any tongue but that of the wolves who are his companions.'

'He runs with wolves?'

'Yes. He is what is the word . . . ?' He said something in his own tongue.

'A feral child,' Benedict translated. 'A child of nature. So how did you find him?'

'He was not always so. His mother brought him to us in Bistrita, when he was not yet three years old, and begged us to take him off her hands. Or perhaps I should not say begged for she was a proud woman and it was more of a command, as if we were there to serve her. And she was prepared to pay for us to relieve her of the burden.'

'She found him a burden, even then,' murmured Benedict, regarding the boy with compassion.

'I am afraid so. A great burden. He did not speak, nor did he appear to hear her or heed her commands. Curses had no effect upon him, nor blows, and I fear he may have had much of both. He lived in a world of his own, and continued to do so even after we took him in and, I do assure you, treated him with far more kindness than his mother. And there were some small signs of a response. We had him examined by doctors – with some difficulty for he does not care to be looked upon by strangers – and they said he suffers from a condition that I think is called, in the English, autism. He is not easy with his own kind, with other people. And in Inger's case I fear it goes much further than that. Yet the doctors say he is not stupid. And he has many other gifts. Indeed, we had a great fondness for him and when we moved from Bistrita we took him with us.'

'And yet, forgive me, Reverend Father, but you let him run wild with wolves?'

The hegemen's eyes clouded. 'What were we to do? He has a madness to be with wild things. Indeed, he seems able to communicate with them. I do not know how this is. We tried at first to keep him from them but it is impossible. The only way is to keep him chained – or leave him to the authorities, who would send him to an asylum. It seems less cruel to let him come and go as he pleases.'

'Even in winter?'

'There are caves that give him shelter. He and his

wolves. He is familiar with the underworld and with the hidden tracks in the mountains. And he knows the door is always open to him here, though sometimes he chooses other means of gaining entry.'

Jade shuddered at the thought of being out in the mountains in those few rags of clothing, but he seemed none the worse for it. He looked fit and well fed, if you looked beyond the dirt and the scars.

'You do not fear that he may come to harm, or be hunted down by those who might consider him to be more suited to an asylum than to the wilderness?'

'Oh, we do fear it. Constantly. But he has strange powers. I do not think he is easy to capture. Or even to be seen if he does not wish it.'

'You have not heard from his mother, since she left him with you?'

'No. Nor did we expect to. She was not the most loving of mothers, I think.'

'And there is no father? Or any other family?'

'Not that we know . . .' His eyes strayed to Jade and there was a question in them. 'But what is your interest in the matter, my son? For I do not think you come upon us by accident.'

'No. I will be honest with you, Reverend Father. We came for the boy.'

238

'Ah.' The hegemen sighed, plucking at his beard with his long yellow fingers. 'And how, may I ask, did you know he was here?'

'Perhaps because he wished it to be known.'

'I see.' He looked towards the boy with a bemused smile. 'I think that might be the case. Our Inger has his own way of communicating, I think, and not only with wolves.'

Jade could still feel the boy's eyes upon her. She returned his stare for a moment, though it made her uncomfortable. It was almost as if he was peering into the very depths of her being. For all his grubbiness, he was the most beautiful boy she had ever seen, but then he moved his head slightly, bringing his face further into the light and she started with surprise and some alarm for she saw not Mowgli, the jungle boy, but Kobal, her father.

'So,' said the hegemen, stroking his beard. 'What do you want with him?'

'I think it is more a question of what he wants with us,' said Benedict quietly.

A picture formed in Jade's mind of a wolf pack running through a forest and then she saw the two human figures running with them. The figures of Inger and herself.

'He wants us to go with him,' she said.

Benedict regarded her keenly for a moment. 'What makes you think that?' he said.

'I don't know. Just a feeling I have.'

'Just a feeling,' he repeated. 'And where does he want us to go?'

And now they were standing on a ridge, looking down on the ruins of a castle and the snow was falling gently. Snow, or ashes. And she remembered the dream she used to have when she was at Saint Severa's.

'Jade?'

'I don't know,' she said, 'but I don't think it's too far.'

'I see. And when does he want us to go on this journey? Now?'

His eyes drifted to the window. It shook with a gust of wind and they saw the flakes of snow dancing in the faint light that penetrated the darkness beyond.

'We can wait until morning,' said Jade after another pause. 'At first light.'

'That's a relief,' remarked Benedict ironically.

'Wherever you are going it will not be alone,' said the hegemen, who had turned to peer through the window into the darkness beyond. 'He will have his friends with him.'

And looking over his shoulder Jade saw the circle of shadowy figures against the white carpet of snow on the forecourt below and the red eyes glinting in the light that spilled from the window.

'See,' said the hegemen, 'they are waiting for you.'

23

Trekking with Wolves

They set off at first light, following a winding trail through the mountains; high above the treeline now, with the monastery far below on its pinnacle of rock and the river a thin wavering line scrawled across the bottom of the valley. There was no sign of Inger's companions of the night before, though their prints were engraved in the crust of snow outside the monastery door. It had stopped snowing and the sun was out but it made little impact on the white powder that dusted the shaded side of the trees and clung to the folds and crevices of the mountain slope: the first stubborn inroads of the winter to come.

The boy led the way, loping ahead of them and waiting impatiently for them to catch up every few minutes or so. Benedict matched his pace to Jade's, who was finding the going hard. She walked head down, stiff and weary from her efforts of the day before, her feet hot and heavy.

She caught Inger looking at her sometimes, while he was waiting for them to catch up, as if he was curious as to what kind of creature she was. She supposed they didn't get many girls in the monastery. Then suddenly she felt he was trying to speak to her. Not speak. Communicate.

A picture formed in her head of taking her boots off and soaking her feet in a cool mountain steam and she was lying back on soft grass with the sun glinting through the branches of overhanging trees. Of course, this could be a thought she had put there herself but there was something in the intensity of his gaze that made her think it came from Inger and that he was trying to comfort her. And amazingly her feet felt better.

She tried to throw thoughts back to him. Pictures of when she had been happy, of things that had made her happy. This was difficult. She realized that she had not been happy, truly happy, for a long time. The images that came to mind were from when she was much younger and they usually involved going on a trip somewhere with Aunt Em: shopping in London or visiting an exhibition or something. But she thought she was getting through to him because different pictures started to form in her mind, pictures that must be coming from him: of the forest and mountains and rushing streams. This picture language was all very well but she didn't know how to frame the questions she wanted to put to him. Like where he was taking them and how far it was. And what it was like to live with wolves.

And the other question she wanted to ask was about Kobal. She wanted to know if Inger had ever met him. She tried forming pictures of Kobal in her mind and projecting them at him but there was no response. Either because he didn't recognize the picture or he didn't want to reveal that he had. She knew they were taking a chance following him into the wilderness. He might so easily be leading them into a trap. But she didn't think so. She could not believe he was a creature of Kobal. There was an innocence about him but also an independence. He was a free spirit. She couldn't believe anyone could control him, even Kobal.

She saw him watching her again and wondered if he knew what she was thinking all the time, or just when they were trying to communicate with each other. It was odd, a bit embarrassing – and certainly frightening – to know someone could read your thoughts whenever they wanted to. And yet she did not feel threatened by it, as she did by Kobal. She felt there was a bond between them, an understanding, and that it was far greater than anything she had felt for any of the other children of Kobal: her half-brothers and -sisters. She felt as if he was reaching out to her, in his way, trying to reassure her that there was nothing to fear. And she wanted *him* to trust *her*. Not to lose his independence but just to trust her, to be her friend.

She'd never had many friends. Not at Saint Severa's and not even at the school she had gone to before that in Turnham Green. She didn't make friends easily. She was too suspicious, too cautious, never sure if she could trust people. Now she thought about it, this seemed a bit like a wild animal. A wolf child. But then she was the Child of the Forest, and that gave her something in common with Inger, too.

She remembered how, when she was a little girl, she used to play at being a wolf. 'I'm Wolf today,' she would announce at breakfast – and that was it: for the rest of the day she was this creature called Wolf. She walked like a wolf, stalked like a wolf, howled like a wolf, even ate like a wolf, when she could get away with it. And her foster parents had to treat her like a wolf. If they forgot and called her Jade she wouldn't answer them. She just gave them a look – a warning look, with a hint of menace in it, showing her teeth – and they would say, 'Oh, I forgot. You're Wolf today. Sorry.'

She had thought at the time – or perhaps when she was a little older – that the wolf was a product of her own imagination . . . but what if it was Inger, even then, putting thoughts into her head?

How could she know which were her own thoughts and which were the thoughts someone else had planted there?

But you could go crazy thinking that.

After they had been climbing for an hour or more and the monastery was lost in the distance Benedict touched her shoulder and she looked up and saw the grey figures watching them from a rocky outcrop a few hundred metres above. Inger's 'companions'. He called to them and they bounded toward him, mobbing him like friendly hounds and then following obediently at his heels, glancing back occasionally at the two figures toiling after them up the mountain. There were six of them. His own six grey brothers and sisters. Jade wondered if he had chosen that number deliberately. She found herself feeling jealous of them, because they were more Inger's family than she was. She imagined what it would be like to live in the forest with Inger, the two of them running wild with the wolf pack, and she wondered if that was a thought he had planted in her head too, and she was pleased with it.

By mid-morning they had reached the long ridge at the top of the valley but there was no hint of rest or respite in the bleak landscape that lay ahead: only more ridges, broken by deep gullies and canyons, and the high peaks beyond. No habitation that they could see, not even a track – for Inger and his wolves followed hidden trails, apparent only to their eyes.

At midday Benedict insisted on a break and he and Jade consumed the simple lunch the monks had prepared for them: flat pitta bread with goat's cheese and olives washed down with a flask of spring water. They offered some to Inger but he just stared at the food and then at Jade. This time there was no picture in her mind but she seemed to know, instinctively, what he was thinking.

'He will not eat while his wolves go hungry,' she said.

On they trekked, up and down the endless, exhausting ridges until at length and to Jade's infinite relief they began to descend into another long valley. Here they entered the treeline again and lost sight of their guide for long periods as they trudged through the silent, gloomy forest. But they could see the trail of paw- and footprints through the carpet of icy snow and they continued to follow them downhill until suddenly they emerged into a small clearing by a stream and saw him, among his wolves, bent over some object on the ground . . . and then one of the wolves moved back a little and she saw that it was a deer, its eyes still open but glazed in death and its throat torn and bleeding. Then Inger bent down and plunged his knife into the body and when he straightened up she saw the raw and bleeding lump of flesh in his hand and she turned away in horror as he lifted it to his mouth.

She caught Benedict's eye.

'Gross,' she said.

'Well, he could certainly use some table manners,' he observed.

'But how did he get like this?'

Benedict shrugged. 'It's what happens if you run with wolves,' he said. 'You eat like wolves.'

'And think like them?'

'Probably.'

This was an altogether less attractive image than the one she had conjured earlier. She hadn't expected him to be a vegetarian – but to plunge his hand into a bleeding carcass and eat the raw flesh . . . She decided that running with the wolf pack wasn't such a great idea after all.

'But how can they have let it happen? The monks, I mean. They were supposed to be looking after him.'

'You heard what the hegemen said. They couldn't stop him. He has a mind of his own.'

She wondered if Inger could sense her disgust, but he seemed to have other things on his mind at the moment. She remembered what Kobal had said. It's no good reading the mind of a serial killer if all he's thinking about is his dinner – unless dinner is his next victim.

'So much for his perfect children,' she said.

'I told you, kids have a way of finding their own identity. He's a child of nature.'

'But what will happen to him if he goes on like this?' she demanded. 'He can't live like this for ever.'

'He doesn't seem to be doing too badly,' he pointed out. 'And none of us can live for ever.'

'Not even you?'

'Not even me. I just have a longer span than most.' He paused and looked up at the sky, or what he could see of it through the trees. 'And perhaps . . .' But he didn't finish. He just shrugged and looked at her and smiled and said, 'Who knows?'

She felt a shiver of alarm.

'What do you mean?'

'Nothing. Intimations of mortality,' he said obscurely. 'But this is where it all began. Perhaps this is where it will end.'

She turned back and looked at Inger and his wolf pack, still feeding on the deer, though there wasn't much left of it now.

'Well, I can't see him lasting much longer,' she sniffed in disapproval. She had a sudden image of her foster mother, who couldn't stand the sight of blood. Blood and bad manners. 'What happens when he gets old? And the monks have all died?'

'Then you'll have to look after him,' he said with a grin.

'Me?' She was shocked.

'He is your brother.'

'I didn't choose him,' she retorted violently.

'None of us choose our own family. Come on, Jade. What are you going to do if we manage to rescue them from Kobal? Walk away from them?'

'I hadn't thought about it,' she confessed. She felt deflated all of a sudden and ashamed. All it needed was to see someone stuffing raw meat into their mouth and she didn't want to know them.

'You're the eldest,' Benedict persisted. 'They're your responsibility in a way.'

The thought of having to look after that lot. She remembered the children in her dream, watching her with their big eyes. As if they expected something of her. As if they were counting on her.

And she did not know what they wanted, or how she was supposed to help them. Or even if she wanted to.

But he was right. Somebody had to look after them.

'What about you?' she said.

'I'm a monk,' he said. 'Monks don't have kids.'

She looked at Inger again. He'd finally finished his meal and was leaning against a tree, his face and arms covered in blood. When he saw her looking at him he belched loudly.

'I think I'll become a nun,' she said.

They continued on their way but only for a short while, until they reached a small stream where the wolves drank their fill. To her surprise and relief she saw Inger splash water over his face and arms, washing away the blood.

'Do you think the monks taught him that?' she asked Benedict.

'I would think they insisted on some basic hygiene,' he said, 'whenever he was in the monastery. Or maybe he's picked up on your sense of disgust.'

'You think so?'

'Well, you haven't been trying to hide it. He wouldn't have to read your mind. He could see it in your face.'

She looked at him again and felt ashamed. He was lolling about with his wolves on the banks of the stream, resting after their meal. She walked over and sat down beside him. The wolves ignored her but it still felt weird to be sitting among a wolf pack. Inger turned and looked at her but she couldn't read his expression. Or his thoughts. But then another picture formed in her head. A picture of a little boy sitting on the floor playing with a toy truck and on his face an expression of such innocence, so intent on his game, so happy, and though his hair was shorter, his face younger, she saw Inger in him.

She reached out a hand and placed it on his. The same hand that had stuffed raw, bleeding flesh into his mouth.

'I'm sorry,' she said. She wasn't entirely sure what she was sorry about. Disgust — or distrust. But he looked at her curiously and she felt a strange warmth inside. Like the feeling she'd had when Aunt Em had put her arms around her in the car on the fells. She remembered something from *The Jungle Book*, the universal greeting that Baloo the bear teaches Mowgli: the master law of the jungle. *We be of one blood, you and I.*

Then she remembered — it was the blood of Kobal.

Then Inger stood up with a graceful ease and she saw the wolf in him again and he made a sound in his throat and the wolves were off their haunches, moving as one, ready to continue on their journey.

By mid-afternoon they had reached the floor of the valley and they followed the course of a small river that came tumbling down from the slopes ahead of them. Jade dreaded the prospect of another climb, but there seemed no alternative for the valley was devoid of habitation or any sign of human life. Then, just as they lost the last light of the sun, they heard a distant but strangely familiar sound. Benedict looked up at the sky, listening, his whole body tense.

'Puma,' he said.

'Puma?' She frowned. It didn't sound like a puma.

'Helicopter. AR 330.'

How did he know these things? A monk from the Middle Ages. She supposed it must be the warrior in him.

Then they saw it. Rising above the crest at the head of the valley and heading in their direction. Jade looked for Inger in alarm but he and his wolves were no longer there. It was as if they had melted into the surrounding forest.

She looked at Benedict again, wondering why he was so still. She was conscious of how exposed they were standing by the side of the river, out of the cover of the trees. Her alarm increased when the machine banked sharply and came swooping down on them.

'What if it's Kobal?' she said.

'It's not Kobal,' said Benedict. 'Not unless he's joined the Romanian army.'

Sure enough, as it came closer, Jade saw that it was

painted a uniform khaki with military markings and as it hovered above them she could see the soldiers peering down. Even so, she could not help thinking they might have been better off hiding in the forest with Inger and his wolves. After all, she was a fugitive travelling under a false passport and any contact with the authorities was to be avoided.

After circling around them for a minute or so, the helicopter came down on a patch of open ground beside the river and four uniformed men jumped out, armed with rifles.

'Stay here,' Benedict instructed her, 'while I go and talk to them.'

So she stayed at a small distance, carelessly throwing stones into the river and watching furtively as he spoke with them. After a short while he came back and said the officer wanted a word with her.

'I had to tell him you were from England,' he said. 'In case he decided to question you. I told him we were on a walking holiday. And now he wants to talk to you — but only to practise his English. There's nothing to worry about.'

Even so, Jade felt decidedly uneasy as she followed him back to the group of soldiers.

'Hello,' said the officer with a polite bow. 'My

name is Captain Andrei Antonescu. I am please to meet you.'

And so it began. For the next few minutes Jade felt as if she was in one of those foreign-language films that teach you basic conversation.

'Where you live in Engaland?'

'I live in London.'

'You like Romania?'

'Yes, I like it very much.'

'I like to visit Engaland. I like to see London. I like to see the Queen. Do you see the Queen?'

'Yes. I see her every morning, putting her washing on the line.'

She felt Benedict's hand on her shoulder, squeezing none too gently.

'I like the English football. You like the English football?'

'Yes, I like football. Which team do you like?'

'David Beckham.' He beamed at her and she nodded and all the other soldiers said 'David Beckham', laughing and nodding.

How long this might have gone on for was anyone's guess but finally Benedict interrupted and spoke a few words in Romanian, pointing at the sky and clearly indicating that they must be on their way, and the captain said, 'Bye bye,' and shook their hands and let them continue.

'Wow.' Jade blew out her cheeks. She used an expression of Aunt Em's. 'A bit more of that and I think I'd have lost the will to live. What are they doing here?'

'Shooting wolves,' he said.

She stared at him. 'Seriously?'

'Seriously. They're on a training exercise but if they see any wolves they shoot them.'

'Is that allowed?'

Benedict shrugged. 'Who knows? But I don't suppose there's going to be much protest in this country – except from the wolves. He says in winter they go down into the valleys and kill sheep.'

'The soldiers?'

'No. The wolves.' He rolled his eyes. 'He warned me to look out for them. He said they could be dangerous.'

The helicopter took off again and they waved as it flew overhead.

'They've got a camp a little way up the river,' Benedict said. 'A whole company of them in tents. I guess we better change our route.'

A few minutes later Inger and his wolves emerged

from the trees. He looked searchingly at Jade. She formed a picture in her mind of the soldiers in their tents, further upriver – and of the helicopter and the guns. He seemed to understand. He looked about him and then up at the slope on the far side of the river.

'What now?' said Benedict.

'We have to cross the river,' said Jade.

This was easier said than done. Inger and his wolves simply plunged into the water and swam to the other side but Benedict didn't want to get their clothes wet. Not with night coming on.

'Do you think he will understand if I throw him the rope?' he asked Jade.

'Understand what?'

'That I want him to tie it to a tree,' he said, rolling his eyes again.

She saw Inger looking back at him and made a picture in her head.

'I think he understands,' she said. 'But I don't know if he can tie a knot.'

'Well, let's live in hope, shall we?' said Benedict.

He uncoiled the rope and tied a rock to one end. Then he swung it round and round his head and let go. It soared across the river and landed at Inger's feet.

He picked it up and sniffed at it curiously. Then he picked it up and made to throw it back.

'No!' shouted Benedict.

'It's all right,' said Jade. She was smiling. 'He's only teasing you.'

'Teasing me?' Benedict stared at her and then at Inger, who was now calmly tying the rope to a tree. He shook his head. 'I'm getting old,' he said.

He tied the rope to a tree on their side of the river so it was stretched taut, about four feet above the water.

'Now what?' asked Jade.

'Have you not done this before?'

She shook her head. 'It wasn't something they taught us at Saint Severa's,' she pointed out. 'The nuns didn't do much swinging from ropes.'

'OK,' he said. 'Watch me.'

He took the rope in both hands and swung his feet up. Then he swarmed over the river hand over hand, hanging backwards over the water. It looked easy.

'Now your turn,' he said.

It was no good. She could just about get her feet up on the rope but she couldn't make them stay there.

'I'm sorry,' she said. She felt such an idiot, especially with Inger watching.

Benedict crossed back to her side of the river. She wondered if he was going to carry her across, but oh no, he had other ideas. He took a length of cord from his pocket. Then he lifted her up and told her to hook her feet around the rope. Then he lashed her feet together.

'Now haul yourself across,' he said. 'But don't let go – or you'll go head first into the water and hang there upside down.'

She thought he was joking.

'Off you go,' he said.

There was a terrible ache in her arms but she daren't let go, the thought of hanging upside down with her head in the water was too horrible. She hauled herself as fast as she could to the other side and then had to hang there a bit longer until Benedict untied the rope.

'There's a lot of Kobal in you,' she said as she stood on solid ground and massaged her aching arms, but she was glad he hadn't carried her across.

'I knew you could do it,' he said with a grin.

They began to climb again, away from the river, with Inger and the wolves running ahead of them. After about half an hour, with the sun now low in the sky, they came to a clearing with a great rock rising high above the surrounding trees. Inger and the wolves were lying in deep shadow at the foot of it but as they approached Jade saw that the shadow concealed the entrance to a cave.

Jade wondered if this was to be their refuge for the night. But Inger looked at her and a different picture formed in her mind. Her heart sank.

Inger turned and led the way into the cave with the wolves at his heels.

Benedict looked at her questioningly.

'Now what?'

'We follow,' she said wearily.

And so they followed, into the darkness.

24

The Ruined Castle

The shadows danced on the walls of the cave in the light of Benedict's torch. Slender rock pillars shaped like cowled monks or mitred bishops, stalactites and stalagmites like prison bars or a vampire's fangs, boulders like trolls and once a shape that Jade could have sworn was the cloaked figure of Count Dracula himself.

And even more weird and wonderful than these, the long shadows of the boy and his wolves moving ahead of them through the rock-and-crystal jungle, never pausing or looking back.

From time to time a passage branched off to left or right but Inger strode confidently through the labyrinth with the wolves at his heels. Benedict took a felt-tip pen from his rucksack and marked the rocks from time to time with a red cross.

'So we can find our way back,' he said, 'if we have to do it alone.'

They crossed stone bridges over deep chasms that betrayed a distant gleam of black water when Benedict shone his torch down. They entered great caverns, splendid underground cathedrals jewelled with crystal, so vast the torch beam could not reach the soaring vaults above. Unlike the catacombs under Paris there was no indication that any humans had been here before, living or dead. And no animals except the wolves.

Then, after they had been trekking for an hour or more, Jade looked up and saw what appeared to be a layer of black fungus on the roof above – until Benedict played his torch on it and she realized with a shock that it was composed of bats. Hundreds, maybe thousands of the creatures, hanging there with their heads tucked into their folded wings. A ripple passed through the assembled ranks as the torchlight panned along them and she thought she heard their high-pitched squeaks of protest. Bats had never particularly bothered her in the past but she shuddered at the thought of them taking fright and descending in a great shrieking black cloud to envelop her in those leathery wings. But it was only a collective twitch in their sleep, a bat nightmare of human intruders creeping through their dark domain. Then she saw that Inger had stopped not far ahead of them, his way obstructed by a wall of what appeared to be solid rock. Then he ducked down and disappeared through a narrow gap at the bottom with his wolves slinking after him one by one.

Jade and Benedict followed on all fours and after a few moments she felt a draught on her face. Then the roof rose above them and she stood up and felt the soft brush of pine needles on her cheek and the kiss of cold, wet snow. And she stepped out on to a forested mountain slope with the snow falling gently from the night sky and a furry slither of moon glowing dimly through the black clouds.

Inger and his wolves were nowhere to be seen but Benedict led the way carefully down the slope until they reached a wide ledge overlooking a long valley hemmed in by tall snow-capped peaks . . . And there, on a spur of rock just below them, lay the ruins of a castle, its decaying ramparts like tombstones against the night sky.

Benedict hauled her back into the shadows and

pressed a finger to his lips. She looked at him in bemusement for the valley seemed deserted. Then she looked again and saw what he had seen: a glimmer of light among the ruins. More than a glimmer: a bonfire, its flames flickering upon the shattered walls and its sparks rising into the air and dancing with the snowflakes above the derelict turrets.

'I think we've found Dracula's lost castle,' murmured Benedict. He was looking down at the ruin with a strange expression on his face, almost fearful. She had never seen him afraid and it scared her. Then he added, 'And I've been here before, a long time ago.'

He seemed to be in a world of his own but he shook his head of whatever memories lingered there and led the way down. He had switched off his torch but there was just enough reflected light from the snow for them to see where they were putting their feet and they moved cautiously down the slope, flitting like shadows from tree to tree.

They reached the outer edge of the castle and passed through a large ragged gap in the walls, creeping silently along the foot of the ramparts. There was still no sign of Inger and his wolves and they could no longer see the bonfire, though they could smell the woodsmoke in the clear night air and something else: the aroma of a rich, meaty stew that made Jade's mouth water and she clenched her stomach to stop it rumbling in protest. Then they rounded a stone buttress and saw the glow of the fire just below them in what had once been some underground dungeon or cellar, now partly open to the sky.

They crept forward and peered down through a gap in the vaulted ceiling and saw several small figures seated in a half-circle around the fire where a large black cauldron simmered and steamed. Jade knew at once who they were, though she could not see their faces, and as if in confirmation, the tall, unmistakable figure of Barmella moved into the firelight and began to stir the cauldron with a large spoon, just like the witch she was. And in the shadows beyond Jade saw a dark hooded figure that she knew must be Kobal.

And next to Kobal, lying on the ground but with her features clearly illuminated by the fire, was Aunt Em.

25

The Children of Kobal

Jade felt Benedict's hand on her shoulder and they moved furtively back from the edge of the roof. Her mind was in turmoil.

'What are we going to do?' she whispered.

'We have to get her away from them, before we do anything else,' he said.

'Aunt Em?'

'Who do you think I mean?'

'She doesn't look like a hostage,' she said.

'What should a hostage look like?'

'Well, more kind of . . . trapped.'

She recalled what Emily had told her on the night train to Budapest about her relationship with Kobal. *We were friends. Of sorts. In fact, I'll be honest with you, we were more than that . . .*

It was the first time it had crossed her mind that she might have gone with Kobal voluntarily. But now she could think of nothing else and it scared her.

'Stick close to me,' said Benedict, 'and don't make a sound.'

He led her off along the ramparts, their footsteps muffled by the snow, until they reached another gap in the roof. It was darker here and they had a better view of the room below. Jade could see the children more clearly now. There was Paco, peering eagerly towards the cauldron on the fire. He had spent much of his early life scavenging on a rubbish dump in Guatemala and he was always hungry. He would be cold, too, Jade thought, away from his Land of Fire. And Shrika, the Child of Magic, far from her own home in India, huddled in a blanket, her eyes glowing like coals in the firelight. It was doubtful if she missed her life in the circus, where she had been practically a slave, but she would miss the sunshine, miss the kites flying in the blue sky, miss the animals, perhaps, and the power she had over them. Jade wondered what she would make of Inger if she ever met him.

The other three were turned away from her but Jade knew who they were. Solomon, the boy soldier from Uganda, Child of the Moon; Kai, from her island in the South Pacific, the Child of the Sea; and Barega, the Child of the Wind, from Arnhem Land in Australia. All far from home. And none of them would be happy in the cold. Or in this bleak wilderness of mountains and snow.

Why had Kobal brought them here, to a ruined castle in the black heart of Transylvania?

She looked across to where he sat in the shadows. She could not see his features under the hood but she knew it was him. She worried that he could sense her watching him in the darkness but he seemed perfectly relaxed, seated by the fire, taking occasional sips from a cup he nursed in both hands. Jade looked up at Aunt Em, beside him, and almost let out a cry. For from this new angle she could see that her hands were tied.

Benedict jerked his head and they moved back from the edge of the ramparts. He put his mouth close to her ear.

'How do you feel?' he said.

She looked at him in surprise. It seemed a strange question to ask in the circumstances.

'Fine,' she said, as you do, even in a ruined castle, in the snow, in the middle of Transylvania. But in fact she felt infinitely better than she had a few minutes earlier. She was not happy that Aunt Em was a prisoner, but it was infinitely preferable to her being a traitor.

'There are some steps leading down from the far side of the ramparts,' Benedict murmured in her ear. 'But we need some kind of a diversion.'

And right on cue they heard the howling of a wolf.

A wolf, or a wolf boy.

Then the whole pack joined in. A fiendish chorus from the darkness above the ruins.

They moved back to the edge of the ramparts and peered down into the room. They were all on their feet, their heads raised towards the sound of the wolves, though it seemed to come from every direction, echoing around the mountain slopes.

Then suddenly Barmella moved, darting off into the shadows and returning with a gun – a rifle, or a shotgun. Jade watched as she broke it open at the breech, inserted a pair of cartridges, and moved off towards the stairs. Kobal followed and Jade saw that he, too, was armed. But not with a gun. Jade was no expert at weaponry but it looked to her like a crossbow and he had a quiver of arrows slung over his shoulder.

Benedict and Jade crouched down as they came running up the stairs and made off along the ramparts into the darkness.

'Look after this,' said Benedict, dumping his rucksack at her feet. Then, before she could say anything to stop him, he dropped straight down from the roof into the room below.

The five children drew back from the crouching figure that had landed among them. He straightened up and stared at them, his gaze moving slowly from one to the other. No one spoke, or made any attempt to raise an alarm, and no one tried to stop him as he walked calmly over to Emily.

Jade saw the flash of steel as he hacked at her bonds with a knife. Then, without taking his eyes off the five children, he backed towards the steps, pulling her with him by the hand.

Jade raced along the ramparts to meet them as they came running up the steps. The air was still filled with the song of howling wolves but now there was a shout from the darkness below and moments later something hit the ramparts with a terrible force not far from their heads, sending chips of stone hurtling in all directions and they heard the sharp report of a gun.

'Go!' Benedict shouted at Jade, thrusting Emily before him along the ramparts. 'Get her out of here. Back to the cave.'

'But what about you . . . ?' she began. Then there was another sound. A kind of tearing sound – as if the air itself had been ripped apart like a piece of cloth – and a sickening thud. She looked around her in bewilderment . . . And then she saw Benedict.

He had stopped dead in his tracks. And now he went down on one knee and bent his head, as if he was praying. Then Jade saw the steel bolt protruding from his chest. A steel bolt from a crossbow.

She ran to him but he pushed her away.

'Go,' he said again. She saw the pain in his face.

'No,' she cried. 'Not without you.'

He smiled then and for a moment she was reassured, remembering what had happened when he was shot in the catacombs.

'I'll be along in a little while,' he said. 'There is something I have to do.'

26

Secrets and Lies

Gasping and sobbing for breath, braced for the sudden, shocking impact of bolt or bullet, Jade and Emily scrambled and clawed their way up the slope above the ruined castle. Jade looked back many times but no one seemed to be following them – and certainly no one was shooting at them, though they must be clearly outlined against the snow. Then they were in among the trees and she followed the footmarks she and Benedict had made on the way down until they reached the rocks and trees at the mouth of the cave.

She had half expected to find Inger and his wolves here but there was no sign of them and she could no longer hear their mournful howls. She looked back once more towards the castle. No movement among those grim, dark stones. Just a few red sparks from the bonfire rising into the still, night air.

Emily had collapsed at the foot of the rocks.

'What now?' she said.

'We wait for Benedict,' said Jade firmly. She was going nowhere without him. But what if he didn't come? She could still see that terrible bolt sticking out of his chest. Somehow it seemed worse than a bullet. And then she remembered something he had told her in the past. Something about being killed by his own kind.

'How did you find me?' asked Emily.

'Inger led us here,' she replied distractedly, still worrying about Benedict.

'Who's Inger?'

'I'll tell you later.' Jade regarded Aunt Em dully. She looked all right. And she was no longer dressed as a nun. 'What about you? What happened on the train?'

'A woman came up to me and said you'd been taken ill . . .'

'Barmella.'

'Yes. Only I didn't know it then. She led me through the station and threw me into a car — and there he was . . .' She shivered suddenly, but not from the cold. 'It's nearly twelve years since I last saw him and he doesn't look a day older.'

'You're beginning to believe it, aren't you?'

'Well, either that or he's got a great beautician.'

'But how did you get here? He can't have driven.'

'He had a helicopter.'

'A helicopter?' Jade suddenly remembered the soldiers. 'Listen,' she said urgently. 'There are some soldiers on the other side of the mountain. They're camped by the side of the river and they've got a helicopter. The name of their captain is . . .' But she couldn't remember his name. 'It doesn't matter,' she said. 'He speaks English. But don't let him talk to you about David Beckham.'

Emily looked mystified. She shook her head. 'What do you mean? Why should he talk to me about—'

'Tell him where we are and we need help. It will only take a couple of hours for you to get through the caves.' She groped in the rucksack Benedict had given her and there was the torch. There were even some spare batteries. And a compass. She had no idea if a compass worked in a cave.

'Keep to the main path,' Jade said. 'You'll see the red marks on the stones every couple of hundred metres.'

'What do you mean? What are you going to do?'

'I'm going to wait for Benedict.'

'Jade, if you think I'm going to leave you here—'

'You have to,' Jade insisted. 'Someone's got to fetch help.'

'OK. So we'll both go.'

Jade shook her head stubbornly. She wondered if she could psych her into it but there were too many rushing thoughts in her brain.

'Jade, if you think I'm going to lose you now . . .' Emily seized her by the shoulders and almost shook her. 'Listen to me. There's something I have to tell you, in case . . .' But she didn't finish. There was a long desolate howl from down below in the valley. Their heads jerked round but they could see nothing.

'You have to go,' Jade insisted once more. 'Now. Before it's too late.'

But Emily wouldn't let go of her shoulders and there was a strange look in her eye. 'I have to tell you this,' she said. 'I may never get the chance again. When I was with Kobal, down there in the castle, he told me something – about when we were working together. Something I swear to you I didn't know until then. Oh, God, how can I put this?'

'You told me you were friends,' said Jade dully. She

didn't want any more confessions of that sort.

'This is something else. To do with our work. He wanted me to . . . to help him with his research. With *our* research. And we needed . . . we needed donors.'

Jade felt the blood drain from her face and she felt faint and ill suddenly because she knew what was coming.

'I was so young and . . . and keen . . . and I thought . . . You have to understand I thought it was so important what we were doing. And it was. We were trying to . . . to . . . It was for the advancement of medical science. To eliminate inherited diseases. To make the world a better place.'

'What are you saying?' But Jade knew what she was saying. 'What did you do?'

'I donated one of my . . . Well, the medical term for it is an ovum but you would call it an egg. For research.'

She still clutched Jade by the shoulders as if she was afraid she would run away but Jade was as still as a statue. And as cold.

'He told me it was for research, babe. I had no idea what he really wanted it for. Oh, Jade, I'm so sorry.'

'You're sorry,' said Jade flatly.

'I mean—'

'Sorry that I was the result.'

'Of course not. Of course not, baby.' She let go of Jade's shoulders and put her hands together as if she was praying. 'I'm just sorry that it happened that way. That you were . . . you were brought into the world that way. Believe me, Jade, I really had no idea what . . . He lied to me.'

'He lies to everyone,' said Jade. 'That's what he does.'

'Yes. Yes I know that. Now.'

'You must have known.'

'No.'

'People said we looked so alike.'

'I just . . . I just put it to the back of my mind. I didn't think it would do any good . . .'

'So you lied to me, too.'

'No. No. I never lied to you, Jade.' She was almost in tears. 'I just never knew how much to tell you.'

'Well, I always wanted to know who my mother was.'

'I promise I'll make it up to you. If we ever get out of here alive.'

'Then go and fetch the soldiers.'

'Not without you.'

'All right.' Jade stood up. Her voice was still

cold. 'Let's do it.' She spoke in conscious imitation of Kobal.

'Both of us?'

'Both of us.'

She scrambled down into the hollow under the rock and pulled aside the small fir shielding the entrance to the cave. 'After you.'

Emily stared at the black hole.

'We have to crawl through that?'

'It gets wider after a bit. Much wider. You can walk upright all the way.'

'Well, you go first.'

'No. You've got the torch and . . . and I'm a bit nervous of caves. I'll be right behind you.'

'You promise?'

'I promise.'

She kept her promise for all of twenty seconds. Then slowly she backed out into the night.

27

The Silver Arrow

Jade picked her way through the stones of the ruined castle. She could still see the shower of sparks reaching up to the sky and when she looked down into the cellar they were all there, gathered around the fire. Kobal and Barmella and the five kids. Except . . . She stared down in astonishment. There were now six of them.

And the sixth was Inger.

How could that be? She could see no sign of his wolves and he did not seem to be a prisoner. She looked for Benedict but could not see him among the group around the fire. She made her way along the ramparts towards the top of the steps where she had left him, fearing what she might find there. But he was not here either. Only a dark stain on the stone floor. And looking down she saw more, trailing down the steps. Then she heard Kobal's voice.

'Jade! Don't stay up there being a party pooper. Come down and join us. We've been waiting for you.'

Slowly, Jade made her way down. And there was Benedict, lying just beyond the light of the fire. She ran over and knelt beside him, staring in horror at the bolt protruding from his chest and the blood that soaked his clothing.

'I told you to go,' he said. It was like a groan.

'What if we pull it out?' she murmured softly. 'Will it heal, like before?'

He gave her a smile that wrenched at her heart.

'Not this time,' he said.

She looked at the bolt again and saw how it shone in the firelight, shone like . . . 'Silver!' she said wonderingly. 'It's made of silver.'

'Yes,' said the voice of Kobal behind her. 'A silver arrow. Shot by his own brother. I think that makes it a double whammy, don't you?'

28

The Angel of the Abyss

'Well, isn't this a sight for sore eyes?' beamed Kobal, spreading his arms in a mock embrace. 'All seven of you. Together at last.'

'It won't be for long,' Jade promised him bitterly.

'Well, for once you might be right about that,' Kobal agreed. 'But just for one night let us savour our moment of togetherness. It has taken me a very long time to achieve this, far longer than I ever imagined. However, here we all are. And a bonus!' He indicated the prone figure of Benedict. 'Uncle Ben is with us. Who would ever have thought it?' He frowned. 'But somehow I don't think *he'll* be staying with us very long, will you, Benbo?'

'A very little time in your company is more than

enough,' Benedict informed him, but in a voice like dry leaves rustling in the wind.

'Oh. Oh.' Kobal clapped his hands. 'Very good. Well, not *very* good but not bad for a monk of the Order of Saint Saviour or whatever it's called these days. Not noted for their sense of humour, the holy warriors,' he informed the others in an undertone. Take themselves far too seriously, if you ask me.' He turned back to Benedict. 'And talking of Orders, what do you think of this lot?' He indicated the children gathered around the fire. 'The new Order of the Dragon. The Draculae. Adorable, aren't they? And gifted? I cannot tell you how gifted these young people are. I fairly swell with paternal pride.'

'I suppose there's a first time for everything,' said Benedict. 'So now they're all here, what are you going to do with them?'

'A good question. An excellent question. What *am* I going to do with them. Such gifted individuals as these. With such enormous potential. Each of them has the capacity to . . . to . . . Oh, I don't know, the possibilities are endless. I will have to sleep on it. We'll all have to sleep on it. Countess – the sleeping bags.'

He clapped his hands again and Barmella strode off into the darkness to return a few moments later with a bundle of sleeping bags.

'Not joining us, Princess?' queried Kobal with a smile. 'Staying out in the cold with your Uncle Ben? Too bad. Never join the losing side. That's my motto in life. Never cast your lot with the losers.'

'Do you mean me?' Benedict demanded weakly. 'Or the whole human race?'

'The human race,' Kobal sneered. 'Where are they racing *to*, do you suppose? And what will they leave behind? A ruined planet. Poisoned seas and polluted skies, burning forests and melting snows. And the heavens littered with their rubbish. Doesn't it make you ashamed, my brother, to be a member of such a team?'

'So who are the winners, Boris?'

'Who are the winners? Another good question. But we will have to wait for morning to find the answer. If you manage to last out the night.'

'Aren't you even going to give him a blanket?' Jade demanded, glaring at him fiercely.

'He doesn't need a blanket. His love of humanity will keep him warm.'

He walked off into the darkness and after a moment Jade ran over to where Barmella had dumped the sleeping bags and found a spare one. She unzipped it all the way round and wrapped it round the wounded man and then lifted up his head very gently and rested it on her legs.

He grinned up at her. 'Welcome to the losing team,' he said, but his face gleamed with sweat and when she put a hand to his brow it was cold.

'Are you in very much pain?' she asked him, wishing there was something she could do.

'Not physical pain. The pain is in my head, or my heart. I was never too sure of the distinction. I'm so sorry to have brought you to this.'

'You didn't. I brought us to it. With a little help from Inger,' she added bitterly. He had probably been acting on Kobal's instructions all along, she thought.

'Don't blame Inger,' Benedict murmured. 'Don't blame any of them. They're in Kobal's power.'

As she had been – and was again.

'What do you think he wants with us?' she asked him.

'I wish I knew. But . . . this place, I know now what it is. It was built by my father.'

'Your father? But you said—'

'I said it was Dracula's castle. But it was here long before Vlad Tepes inherited it.' He coughed and brought up flecks of blood. She had never seen him weak and helpless and it broke her heart. But then he seemed to recover a little. 'Let me tell you a little of our family history,' he said, 'before it's too late.'

'Don't speak if it hurts,' she urged him.

'This is something you should know.' He paused as if to gather his thoughts. His breath was harsh and seemed to come bubbling up as if through water. 'My father was an Austrian knight, Conrad von Ullman, Grand Master of the Order . . .'

'The one who fell in love with the gypsy.'

'Yes. And it was he who built this castle. Above the gateway to Hell.'

'But the castle in Finland, that was supposed to be above the gateway to Hell . . . and the catacombs in Paris . . .'

'There are seven gateways to Hell, according to legend, hidden in various parts of the world. This was believed to be one of them.' He paused for a while, fighting for breath. 'There was a pit leading deep into the ground. So deep no one knew where it ended. The locals called it the Abyss of Abaddon. The pit from which the Dark Angel would emerge, at the end of days.' He smiled at her, though it was more of a grimace. 'Perhaps my father thought that by building a castle here he would be able to stop the Beast from getting out. Or perhaps he had a different purpose. Certainly, I believe Kobal does . . .'

He reached for her hand.

'I have to tell you this, because you have to be ready . . . and you cannot afford to worry about me. You're not here by accident. He brought you here for a purpose. I think he means to sacrifice you. His perfect children. To Abaddon, the Angel of the Abyss.'

29

The Secret of the Septagram

A pale grey light crept through the ruins. Jade stirred and awoke. For a moment she was confused, wondering where she was and how she had come to be here. Then she gave a despairing cry. She looked down at the man she had intended to guard through the night, gripped by the terrible fear that he had died while she slept. But he opened his eyes and smiled. It was a smile shot through with pain and it drove a dagger into her heart, but it was a smile all the same.

'Still with you,' he said. 'Haven't gone yet.' His voice was no more than a wheeze from deep within his chest.

'Just hang on a little longer,' she murmured, for she

had still not given up hope of saving him. 'Aunt Em has gone for help. The soldiers we met—'

'Shhhh . . .' he whispered. 'Don't even think about it.'

'I'm sorry.' She looked about her guiltily. The others seemed still to be sleeping, though she could see no obvious sign of Kobal or Barmella. The fire was a heap of glowing ashes in the corner of the room. It was no longer snowing and the patches of sky she could see through the holes in the roof were turning from grey to pearl.

Benedict raised himself a little and seemed to want to speak. Jade bent her head towards him.

'If they come . . . try to find the crossbow . . . and a silver bolt.'

'But—'

He reached out a hand and gripped her fiercely by the shoulder. 'Bring them to me.'

'I will,' she said, though it was futile to imagine he could use them, even if she could get them from Kobal. 'But I wish there was something I could do for you,' she said.

'Bring me a little water, if you will. And look around for that bow.'

'Rise and shine, the morning's fine . . .' Kobal had

appeared. Wrapped in some outlandish robe, like the Wizard of Oz. It was midnight-blue, Jade saw, with all kinds of designs upon it . . . prominent among them his own sign of the Septagram, the seven-pointed star.

'The first morning of your new life,' he assured them as they reluctantly stirred from their slumber. 'And lo, here comes the sun.'

A sudden beam of light had found a gap in the ruined walls. It struck the floor of their dungeon like a golden lance.

'And see what it reveals,' said Kobal, capering like some stage demon with his arms raised and his robes flaring around him. He seemed to be looking at something on the floor, or dancing around some pattern that he had found there, and as the children clambered wearily from their sleeping bags, Jade's curiosity got the better of her and she left Benedict for a moment to see what it was.

At first she could perceive nothing but then, as her eyes grew accustomed to the light, she saw that in the middle of the room, well away from the ashes of the fire, there were some marks on the floor.

'The Septagram,' declared Kobal, and his voice was no longer mocking. He seemed almost awed. Yet it seemed to Jade to be no more than a simple drawing, a seven-pointed star inside a circle, etched in the stone with some sharp tool or weapon and about two metres across from point to point.

Kobal clapped his hands. 'Come. Up, up. Countess, if you please! There is no time to lose.'

Barmella had appeared, dressed normally – or at least normally for her – in a black ski-suit. She began to shepherd the sleepy children towards the circle on the stone floor.

'To your points,' Kobal commanded them. 'Quickly now, quickly.' He glanced up towards the roof. 'Come on, you all know your points.'

He was like some frantic games organizer at a holiday camp. What on earth was he up to? She remembered Benedict's warning of the night before. He meant to sacrifice them. To the Angel of the Abyss. Whatever that was. In the clear light of day it seemed even more ludicrous than the night before. She looked around for the crossbow but there was no sign of it.

'That's right, Paco. Good boy. My Child of the Sun. Come on, Solomon. See if you can find the Moon. That's it, that's it, good boy, good boy.'

Jade looked at him sharply to see if this was some

elaborate charade but he appeared to be serious. She had never seen him so intense. Or nervous.

Now Jade saw the signs scrawled inside each point of the star. Sun, Moon, the wavy sign of the Sea . . . Something that could be a tree, which must be her own sign of the Forest . . . Others were more obscure . . . A kind of shell, like a conch, was that the Wind? But what was Magic? What was the Spirit? Kai and Barega were looking confused. Shrika sullen. Inger seemed to be casting about as if for a scent or looking to see if he had a tail.

Jade almost laughed. It was absurd. Madness. How could anyone take this madman seriously, least of all himself?

'Inger – come along – see if you can find it. That's right, over here.'

'He can't understand you,' Jade told him wearily. 'He thinks he's a wolf. He can't understand a word you're saying and he can't speak.'

'Of course he can speak, can't you, old son?'

'Yes, Father,' said Inger.

Jade stared at him. *Yes, Father*. In English. Had Kobal coached him? She watched as he obediently took his place in the circle. What a traitor! Now there was only her.

Kobal was looking towards her.

'Well? We're waiting,' he said.

'If you think I'm going to join in your stupid games . . .'

Barmella took a stride towards her.

'No,' Kobal commanded her. 'She must come of her own free will. That is the way it has to be. They must all come of their own free will.'

'Then you'll have to wait a long time,' said Jade defiantly.

Kobal inclined his head as if in thought. Then he turned and walked over to the far corner of the room and bent down over something hidden in the shadows.

The crossbow!

Jade watched in alarm as he fitted another silver arrow into the slot. Then he lifted the weapon to his shoulder and aimed it at the wounded figure on the floor.

'No!' screamed Jade, moving to put her own body between them, but now Barmella leaped forward and seized her in an iron grip.

Kobal lowered the crossbow. 'Well? Now are you going to play our little game?'

'You call that free will?' Jade cried as Barmella

pushed her towards the middle of the room.

'Oh, it will do, I think,' said Kobal in the familiar mocking tones. 'The theological lines are blurred.'

Jade took her place on the seven-pointed star and, though it could have been her imagination, she was convinced the stone floor trembled as if it was thin pinewood planks.

'Good. Very good. Now join hands.'

Reluctantly, Jade took the hands of Paco and Solomon, the two she disliked most. She caught the eye of Shrika and to her surprise she saw that she looked scared. She had never seen Shrika looking scared.

'This is the moment we have been waiting for,' said Kobal. 'In my case, for a long, long time.' He had put down the crossbow and he was standing on a small stone platform, like a pedestal, in the full glare of the rising sun. 'This is your moment in history, my children, the moment you were born for. This the dawning of the Age of Abaddon. The Final Days.'

'He's mad,' Jade muttered for the benefit of the others – and herself. But she was scared now. Benedict was right. Kobal *was* mad and they were to be sacrificed to his insane belief in the dark Angel of the Abyss.

'Now, all you must do is speak your names. Remember your names? Not the names you were given at birth, not the names your mothers gave you. Not even the names of the Septagram. Your *real* names. Your spirit names. The names of your demons.'

Jade felt the blood drain from her face as she remembered. The name he had whispered to her once, on the frozen lake in Lapland, when they were attacked by the reindeer herders.

'Thou art Astoreth, my child of the forest, and I give you the power of Beleth and of Carnivean and of Gaderel. I give you the power of Agaren and of Uzziel. I give you the power of Arakiba.'

Something was happening here, something weird and sinister that she didn't understand and it made her very afraid.

And now they were shouting their names, one by one. Some reluctantly, some with a degree of enthusiasm. Paco, as if he was making fun of the whole thing . . .

'Beleth . . .'

'Carnivean . . .'

'Gaderel . . .'

'Agaren . . .'

And the earth trembled. This was not her

imagination. A tremor had shaken the ground at her feet, like the first warnings of an earthquake, and looking down she saw the cracks appear, following the lines etched in the stone. Was this something Kobal was doing, playing tricks with her mind, or was it for real? She looked across at Shrika — she looked terrified. But her lips moved as if she could not help herself and formed a word. A whisper of a word.

'Louder,' Kobal commanded.

'Arakiba!' Shrika gasped as the cracks widened and spread to the point on which she was standing.

'And now my Child of the Forest . . .'

Jade tried to look round towards Benedict but she could not move her head. Smoke or dust was rising from the cracks. She felt a terrible pain behind her eyes.

'Astoreth,' she groaned.

'Louder. He cannot hear you.'

'Astoreth!'

Another crack. Spreading from her feet to join the others. The sun lanced through the smoke but there seemed to be darkness all around. She closed her eyes.

'Inger. My Child of the Spirit. Yours is the final honour.'

Silence.

'Inger!'

And then Jade heard it. The howl of a wolf.

She opened her eyes and gazed across the circle to where Inger was standing. He threw back his head, his lips drawn back from his teeth. And once more came that loud, defiant howl.

The spell was broken. Kobal jumped down from his pedestal and strode furiously towards the boy. And then Jade heard another sound.

The sound of a helicopter.

Kobal stopped in his tracks and looked up towards the roof. For the only time since Jade had known him, perhaps the only time in his life, he looked bewildered.

Barmella was already making for the stairs, gun in hand, and Kobal followed her, but there was something unsteady in his gait, as if he was drunk.

Jade broke free of the circle and made a beeline for the crossbow. She snatched it up from the floor and ran back with it to Benedict.

'Well done!' He struggled to sit up. 'Put my back against the wall.'

She dragged him across the floor a little so he was propped up against the wall but his face was the colour of death. She did not think he had the strength to raise the weapon, much less fire it.

'Let me,' she said, though she did not know if she could. Not kill someone. Not even Kobal.

'No,' he said. 'Go and see what's happening outside.'

She ran up the stairs. The rest of them were spread along the ramparts gazing upward and she saw the helicopter for the first time, circling the ruins as if it was looking for somewhere to land. Kobal stood with his hands on the parapet staring fixedly towards it and she knew he was using the power of his mind to confuse the pilot: to have him fly in useless circles, or straight into the side of the mountain.

'No!' she screamed at him. But no mere words could stop him. She had to use her mind. She forced her brain to focus. What were his weaknesses? He had none. Then they came to her, out of nowhere, and she hurled them at him like darts of pain. A child snatched from his mother's arms. Before that – before the arms could even hold him. And the young mother, condemned to death as a witch, burning in the flames. *Help me! Help me!* Kobal put his hands to his head and she heard his tortured scream. He turned toward her, an anguished, imploring gaze and she saw the boy in him and relented – relented and released him. And he turned back with a snarl towards the chopper.

Then suddenly the wolves were there.

They came leaping over the ruined walls, Inger's wolves, all six of them, snapping and snarling at him, pulling him by his gorgeous robe, bearing him to the ground . . . And Jade ran to him, not knowing what she was doing or why. She saw Barmella raise the gun to her shoulder and fire both barrels – but not at her or the wolves. Her target was the helicopter, swooping in low over the walls.

There was a burst of automatic rifle fire and Jade dived for cover as the ramparts exploded in a hail of flying stone. When she looked up she saw Barmella lying across the battlements like a broken doll. Jade stared at her, too shocked to take in what had happened, thinking instead of the rag doll she had thrown against the wall in a fit of childish rage. Then a figure darted past her and she saw that it was Inger. Inger, who was no traitor but who had saved them all. She called out to him and he turned and looked at her. And there was something in his expression that she would never forget. A look of intelligence and regret – and a knowledge deeper than hers. And suddenly she knew what was in his mind.

Kobal might be diverted or delayed but he could not be killed, not by wolves or mortal men, and as long as there were seven of them he would carry out his evil plan . . .

And there was only one way to stop him . . .

Then, with cold deliberation, Inger picked up the gun, the gun that was no longer loaded, and stood up and brought it to his shoulder and pointed it at the helicopter.

'No!' Jade screamed as she hurled herself toward him. But once more the ramparts dissolved in a fury of flying splinters and she dived for cover, shielding her head with her arms. She heard the spiteful bark of the automatic rifles as the helicopter howled overhead and when the shooting had stopped and the dust had settled and she looked up, Inger was no longer there.

There was a howl from the ramparts. But not from any wolf. The wolves lay dead or wounded, either from the bullets of the soldiers in the helicopter or some power of Kobal's that had vanquished them before they could tear out his throat. The howl came from Kobal. He was staring down into the room below, his face twisted in an agony of rage and despair. He staggered off towards the stairway and

Jade followed, dreading what she would find.

Inger's body lay at the edge of the Septagram in a spreading pool of blood. His eyes were open but sightless, staring up towards the gap in the roof and the open sky above, and as Jade recoiled in horror, one of his wolves, hurled down from the battlements and terribly wounded, crawled across the floor towards him and began to lick his face. Then, with a great crack, the star split down the middle and fell away to reveal a gaping hole in the floor and there was a roar like thunder from deep within the abyss.

The room was filled with dust or smoke but still the sun lanced through and by its eerie light Jade saw Kobal stumble forward and stand on the edge of the black hole. He stretched out his hands in a gesture that was almost imploring, as if he were trying to excuse himself, and he called out in a language Jade did not understand, save for the one word: '*Abbadon.*' And then she heard another sound, a sound she had heard once before – a violent swish and a thud – and he staggered back a step and she saw the silver arrow in his chest.

Then with a great effort he lurched forward and toppled into the abyss.

Jade stared for a long moment through the haze,

unable to believe that he had gone. Then she ran down the steps to Benedict. He lowered the crossbow and smiled wearily at her.

She lifted up his head gently and cradled it in her arm, stroking his hair back from his forehead but he was so cold, so deathly cold.

'It's over,' he murmured wearily, but there was satisfaction in his voice. 'It's been a long time, but it's over.'

He began to claw at his throat and she saw he was trying to pull out a chain that hung around his neck, part hidden beneath his sweater. She pulled it out for him and saw that it supported a black enamel pendant with a white cross, the emblem of the Knights of Saint Saviour. He smiled at her once more and clenched it tightly in his fist and whispered something to her that she didn't hear. Then he closed his eyes and his head fell back and he died.

30

All Souls

Jade laid her flowers on the stone floor of the college chapel. Snowdrops, the first of the English spring.

The words carved into the stone were in Latin but she knew what they meant because the man standing at her side had told her.

Benedict Ullman, Knight of the Order of Saint Saviour of Antioch, Fellow of All Souls College, Oxford.

But there was no date of birth. Or death.

'He had it done when he first came here in 1438,' said the professor, 'shortly after the college was founded. Or so he told me. He said he wanted to book his place, as it were.'

'1438,' repeated Emily dully. She still couldn't

come to terms with the strange life and death of the man known as Brother Benedict. It offended her sense of order. She was inclined to think of it all as an elaborate hoax. And now this grey-bearded academic seemed to be a part of it. 'And you're telling me he has been here ever since?'

'Well, he came and went,' said the professor. 'But we always kept a room for him, high in the roof. Most people thought he was a ghost.'

'And this didn't seem to bother them at all?'

'Oh, the Fellows are a tolerant lot on the whole, with one or two exceptions. And of course, quite a few of them are ghosts.'

They walked across the quadrangle towards the refectory.

'So he's laid to rest at last,' Professor Higgins reflected, 'in the one place he thought of as home. And now we really will have his ghost to haunt us.' He stopped suddenly and his eyes misted over. 'The times we walked through this quad together. He was my closest friend, you know, for over thirty years. Not long by his standards, but a fair chunk by mine.'

They walked on into the refectory. The table was laid with silver and though it was not dark the candles were lit.

'Shepherd's pie followed by jam roly-poly,' said the professor. Jade looked up at him in surprise – for it was straight from the menu at Saint Severa's. 'His favourite meal. Just as he ordered. With one of his favourite clarets to help it down,' he added for Emily's benefit, with a wink.

'*He* ordered?' Jade frowned. 'You mean Benedict?'

'Oh, yes, he had it all arranged. Not only the tombstone.'

'So he must have known . . .'

'I'm not sure he *knew*, precisely, but he certainly prepared for it. It was all written down in the will. I believe I told you that I was appointed the sole executor of his estate.'

'I didn't know monks had estates,' said Emily. 'I thought they swore a vow of poverty.'

She considered the large portion of shepherd's pie that had been placed before her as if she was wondering how it had got there and what she was supposed to do with it.

'Let me pour you some of this excellent claret,' offered the professor. 'These were warrior monks, remember. Knights, who needed to keep a small army of retainers. And a good cellar. However, he had no property, in the landed sense, and no shares in the stock market so I do not think we can accuse him of exploiting the masses. The money he had acquired over the years was invested mainly in art. Paintings, sculptures, a few rather splendid chess sets, and some rare pieces of porcelain – and of course wine.' He filled his own glass and inspected it appreciatively in the light of the candles. 'The lawyers will doubtless possess a full inventory and doubtless, being lawyers, a precise idea of its value. Though even they may not be able to put an exact price on a Titian.'

Emily choked on her wine.

'Excuse me,' she said, when she could speak. 'Did you say . . . ?'

'A Titian, yes. He had two or three of the smaller works. Apparently he and Tiziano were good friends in the thirties. The 1530s, that is. Then there's the Botticelli, the Donatello and a couple of pieces by Fra Angelica. There's a bit of a gap after the Renaissance. I expect it was a hard act to follow but he took up collecting again in the nineteenth century. He has some very good Pre-Raphaelites and a few pieces by the French impressionists, including at least one Monet . . . Oh, and some early Picassos. He had what you might call catholic tastes.' He chuckled at his own joke and sampled the wine with evident pleasure.

'But . . .' Emily was still staring at him. 'But you're talking *millions*.'

The professor threw his head back and laughed. 'My dear, the wine collection is worth millions. We're talking *hundreds* of millions. And with the exception of a few generous endowments to charities, it's all left to Jade.'

Emily went pale. Even Jade looked up from the shepherd's pie, which she'd been quite enjoying until now. It was a lot more appetizing than the food at Saint Severa's and she entertained high hopes of the jam roly-poly. She seemed to have inherited Benedict's appetite, too.

'I'm sorry,' said Emily, 'but are you playing games with us?'

'I assure you, my dear, I would not be so ill-mannered. The lawyers will have the complete details, which they will doubtless disclose to you during the formal reading of the will, but I thought I should alert you. So you might prepare yourselves. There are certain conditions to be met.'

'Why did he leave all this stuff to me?' Jade enquired sharply.

'Because, my dear, he had to leave "all this stuff" to someone and apparently he had a fondness for you.

You are, of course, his niece and he had no children of his own.'

'Then – he must have trusted me. I mean, he can't have thought I was bad.'

'I'm sure he didn't think that,' said the professor gently.

'You said there were certain conditions to be met,' Emily prompted.

'Oh, nothing alarming. The property is to be held in trust until Jade reaches the age of twenty-five. You and I are named as chief executors . . .'

'Me?'

'You are the mother, I believe,' the professor pointed out delicately. 'And he has stipulated that if any of the items are to be sold it must be on the condition that they continue to be enjoyed by the general public, not hidden away in a vault or some private collection. Most are at present on loan to public galleries. It doesn't apply to the wine, of course. Fortunately.'

He drained his glass and reached for the bottle. Emily shook her head.

'And then, of course, there are the other children.'

'The other children?'

'Your half-brothers and -sisters,' he said to Jade. 'I

understand there are five of them.'

Jade nodded, thinking of Inger. They had buried him in the cemetery at the Monastery of the Holy Spirit at the edge of the forest, where he would be closest to his beloved wolves.

'And they're in Romania at present?'

'The Romanian authorities took them into care,' Emily confirmed. 'Until it was decided what was to be done with them.'

'Do they have homes to go to?'

Jade shook her head.

'Well, the decision is yours, of course, but the funds are available if you should decide to bring them to England. Or establish them anywhere else in the world.'

'He said I might have to look after them some day.'

'Benedict?'

'He said I couldn't walk away from them. I think we should bring them here,' she said to Emily. 'If they want to come.'

'Even Paco?'

'Even Paco.' But she pulled a face. 'We can keep him in a cage and poke sticks through the bars.'

'I think a good school might be a better idea.'

'That's what I mean.'

The professor raised his glass and studied the play of candlelight in its depths. 'Benedict would say there's good in everybody,' he remarked, 'if you looked deeply enough. Mind you, he might have meant it ironically.'

'I miss him,' said Jade.

'So do I,' said the professor. 'So do I.'

'You don't think he was a ghost, do you?' she said.

'Oh, no, not at all,' he assured her. 'He was as much a physical presence as I am. Well, you must know that.'

'So . . . how do you explain it?' demanded Emily with a frown.

'What?'

'Him. And . . . everything.'

'I don't,' said the professor. 'It's a mystery. You can't find the answer to everything, you know, no matter how much you modern scientists might aspire to it.'

Emily had the grace to blush and Jade caught her eye and grinned. She had rather taken to the professor. She hoped they'd see more of him.

'The older I get, the more I'm inclined to appreciate mysteries,' he said. 'And I speak as a Professor of Criminology.' He regarded Jade quizzically over the rim of his spectacles. 'So what about you, young lady — what do you intend to do with your life? Now you are a woman of fortune.'

Jade frowned. 'Dunno,' she said.

The professor threw back his head and roared.

'Good answer,' he said. 'Keep it a mystery as long as you can. Know what Benedict would have advised?'

'Go on.'

'Read lots of books,' he said. Then after considering for a moment, 'And take up kickboxing.'